P9-BZQ-563

Searching for David's Heart

A Christmas Story

Cherie Bennett

AN
APPLE
PAPERBACK

SCHOLASTIC INC.
New York Toronto London Auckland Sydney

For Jeff, my partner in art as well as in life;
those who know us best know how true this is.

ISBN 0-590-30673-1

24 23 22   8 9/0

Printed in the U.S.A.   40

First Scholastic printing, September 1998

ACKNOWLEDGMENTS

In addition to Scholastic, the author gratefully acknowledges the assistance of the following people and institutions:

- —Appleton, WI, Historical Society and Houdini Museum
- —Appleton, WI, Public Library
- —Wisconsin State Patrol, Madison, WI
- —Fr. Fernand J. Cheri III, member National Black Catholic Clergy Caucus, St. Vincent de Paul Church, Nashville, TN
- —Rev. Forrest Harris, Pleasant Green Missionary Baptist Church, Nashville, TN
- —Rabbi Stephen Fuchs, Congregation Beth Israel West Hartford, CT
- —Angela Cowser, Tying Nashville Together (TNT)
- —Vanderbilt University Children's Hospital, Transplant Unit
- —United Network for Organ Sharing, Richmond, VA
- —The Long Wharf Theatre, New Haven, CT

ABOUT THE AUTHOR

Cherie Bennett writes often on teen themes. Her
recent stage adaptation of this novel, *Searching
for David's Heart,* was a winner of the biennial
New Visions/New Voices '98 youth-and-family
theater festival at The Kennedy Center, Washing-
ton, DC, while her *Anne Frank & Me* was pro-
duced off-Broadway to a rave review in the *New
York Times.* She writes both paperback (*The
Bridesmaids, Girls in Love, Sunset Island* series,
Teen Angels series) and hardcover fiction (*Life in
the Fat Lane*) for young people, and also authors
the Copley News Service syndicated teen advice
column "Hey, Cherie!"

1

"I don't see why Mrs. Pritcher is making us give stupid speeches in front of the entire class," I groaned to my big brother, David, and my best friend, Sam Weiss. David was sitting on my bed. Sam was lolling against the closed door of my room, tying his sneakers to each other.

"Because she's malevolent," Sam said calmly. "Adjective. Wishing harm to others."

"Come on, Darce, I bet your speech is great," David said.

I made a face at him. "You think everything I write is great."

"So do I," Sam chimed in, trying to walk with his shoelaces tied together. He fell down.

I looked down at the sheet of notebook paper in my hands. "I'm never going to be able to do it. Never."

"Try picturing our entire class in their underwear." Sam untied his sneakers and reached for the bag of caramel corn on the nightstand.

1

David laughed. "Listen, Darce, you can do this. I know you can."

"*How* do you know?"

He grinned. "Because I know you better than anyone else in the world, don't I?"

"Yeah," I admitted. I peeked at my big brother and nervously scuffed my sneaker into the carpet. "But . . . it's kind of embarrassing to give this speech in front of you."

"How come?"

I couldn't tell him. Anyway, if I read the speech out loud, he'd find out soon enough.

"Hey, I know," Sam exclaimed. "I'll introduce you. It'll help build your confidence."

He put down the caramel corn and scrambled up from the floor. Sam is the shortest and skinniest person in our entire sixth-grade class, so he didn't have that far to go. He cleared his throat dramatically.

"Ladies and gentlemen," he began, holding his clenched right hand just under his mouth as if it were a microphone, "animals, vegetables, and minerals —"

"Vegetables and *minerals*?"

"You don't think some of the kids in our class are lower life-forms?" Sam asked.

"Good point," I agreed.

"Thank you." He cleared his throat again. "You know her, you love her, give it up for . . . Darcy Deeton!"

Sam made the sounds of a crowd cheering. David clapped and whistled.

"Dee Dee! Dee Dee! Dee Dee!" they began to chant.

"You guys?"

"Yuh?" Sam asked.

"Shut up."

They did.

I took a deep breath and let it out slowly. "'The Person I Admire Most,' by Darcy Deeton, Mrs. Pritcher's class, Grade 6-C, Appleton West Middle School."

Sam nodded. "Very thorough."

I shot him a look and he pretended to zip his mouth shut. Then I read my speech:

I cried the first time I saw the ocean. And not because it was so beautiful, either. In June we went to Destin, Florida, on our first family vacation that wasn't to a relative's house. The reason I cried when I saw the ocean was, I knew my dad was going to make me try to swim.

When I was four I fell into a swimming pool and almost drowned. Before that, maybe I was brave like the rest of my family, but I can't remember that far back. All I know is, after that day was when I started to be afraid of things. Water. Heights. Small spaces where you can't breathe. Even giving this speech.

My dad is very brave and he hates cowards. He says all a person needs to get over her fear is willpower, so I really tried. But when he held me in the ocean and ordered, "Put your head under!" I got this terrible, scary feeling. I pushed him away, thrashing around, and suddenly my mouth filled with water, and my lungs. There was no air.

I sucked in, praying for air, but there was just more water, and I was drowning all over again, like when I was four.

The next thing I knew, I was lifted into the sunlight. Smiling down at me was my big brother, David. The sunlight gleamed off his goldish-colored hair. He's perfect on the outside and perfect on the inside, too. But not in an obnoxious way, in a wonderful way.

My father waded out of the ocean. Even from behind I could tell he was disgusted with me, and I felt so bad. But then David smiled at me. I leaned against him and felt his heart beating, and the bad feelings went away.

He told me everything was okay, and that when I was ready, he would teach me how to swim. I got this wonderful, safe feeling. Right then I thought how lucky I am to have David as my brother. He makes everything okay for everybody, but for me most of all. And he believes in me even when I don't believe in myself. That is why he is the person I admire most. Thank you.

My hands felt clammy. The notebook paper was moist where I was clenching it. I snuck a peek at David. He had the biggest smile on his face.

"Darce . . . wow."

"Is that a good 'wow'?" I asked tentatively.

"You're the one in the family with the vocabulary," he said. "But that speech . . . that's about the nicest thing I ever heard in my life."

Happiness spread across my face like sunshine. David got up, hugged me, and swung me in a circle. "My baby sister rules!"

"Agreed," Sam said. "And when all the morons in our class hear you give that speech, they're all going to know how talented you are."

"Cool," David agreed, as he set me down.

Not cool. *So* not cool, in fact, that just the thought of it made me feel sick to my stomach.

I sat on my bed. "What if . . . what if I stutter? And everyone laughs at me?"

"No way," David insisted.

"No one with a brain would laugh," Sam agreed. "And if the vegetables and minerals laugh, it doesn't count."

It counted to me. Especially since the vegetables and minerals in our class laughed at me all the time. For the zillionth time I wondered why it was that when I was with David or Sam, I could be my real self, but with everyone else I turned into this tongue-tied little dweeb.

It was bad enough being the *second*-shortest,

skinniest person in the entire sixth-grade class, but did I have to be the quietest, too? And you would think that if God was going to give me boring, fly-away brown hair, and *freckles*, and a chest that would never even need a training bra because it would never have anything to *train*, He wouldn't have also made me shy *and* tongue-tied, and — this was the worst of all — when I was really nervous, made me *stutter*?

There had to be some mix-up.

I figured that somewhere on planet Earth, there was an about-to-turn-twelve-year-old girl walking around with great everything — looks, curves-in-training, and personality — just to balance out what I lacked.

"Maybe I'll get lucky, and I'll wake up tomorrow with the flu so I don't have to go to school," I said hopefully.

I tried out a few coughs.

"Not very convincing," Sam decided. He upended the bag of caramel corn and poured the crumbs into his mouth.

"You have to believe in yourself, Darce," David said earnestly. "Then you can do anything."

I threw myself back on my bed and stared up at the ceiling. "That sounds like one of those barfy inspirational posters in your team's locker room."

"I'll tell you what I do when I'm scared," David said.

I sat up. *"You? Scared?"*

David nodded. "Sure. Like, take the game tomorrow night. We're playing Manitowoc, right? They were undefeated last year. They play dirty. So I just stare their linebackers in the eyes and *pretend* I'm not scared. If I pretend hard enough, I pretend myself right out of the fear. And run right past 'em."

"Great," I said dubiously. "I'll remember that next time I suit up."

David laughed and pulled on a hunk of my hair. He looked at his watch. "Oh, man, I'm late. I've gotta run."

"But I thought you were going to watch us do our great escape trick," Sam reminded him.

"Can't," David said. "Another time, guys."

"Got a hot date?" Sam asked, comically wriggling his eyebrows.

"Something like that," David said, grinning.

"Oh, really?" Sam asked. "Is this the Big L? As in la-la-la love?"

"I'm so sure," I snorted.

David had dated lots of different girls, but he'd never been serious about any of them. He'd always told me *I* was his favorite girl.

David grinned. "Could be." He kissed my cheek. "Hey, tell Dad I won't be home for dinner. See ya." He loped out of my room.

"Excellent bro'," Sam said, shaking his long, brown hair out of his eyes.

"I know."

Sam didn't have any brothers or sisters. I would gladly have given him my ten-year-old brother, Andy, who was as obnoxious as David was wonderful, but Sam couldn't stand him, either.

I nudged Sam's shoulder. "So, let's hear *your* speech."

Sam rolled his eyes, and gave his speech from memory.

> The person I admire most is The Great Houdini. He grew up right here in Appleton, Wisconsin; we're both Jewish, and we both had the same last name, Weiss, before he changed his to Houdini. Coincidence? I think not. He was the greatest magician and escape artist who ever lived. That is, until me, The Great *Sam*dini.
>
> I am mastering all his tricks, and someday, when I am even more famous than he was and all you mere mortals who ever laughed at me are clamoring for my autograph for which, by the way, I will charge *beaucoup* bucks, I will owe it all to him, my mentor, Houdini. Thank you.

"What does bow-koo mean?" I asked him.

"It's French for *mucho*. I'm teaching myself French on my computer."

"A mentor is a teacher, right?"

"Noun. A trusted advisor."

It figured that he knew. Sam reads the dictionary for light entertainment. And he remembers everything he reads.

"Hey, got any more caramel corn?" he asked hopefully.

"You just ate the whole bag, Sam."

"Cookies? I'll settle for anything with white sugar."

Sam's parents only had healthy food at his house. He hated healthy food.

"You scarfed the cookies yesterday," I reminded him.

He jumped up and went rummaging in my closet. He dragged out a beat-up trunk my dad had used for scout camp when he was a boy, to which he had made certain invisible adjustments. "Let's work on the trick. We'll show it to David next time."

"How can Houdini be your trusted advisor if he's dead?"

"I told you before, Deed, I commune with his spirit. Time for Metamorphosis."

"Noun. A change of form or character," I quoted.

"Excellent recall," Sam approved.

Metamorphosis is the name of Houdini's most famous trick, which Sam was teaching to me. At Appleton Center, in the place where Houdini's house used to be, there's an outdoor sculpture called Metamorphosis. Sam likes to go sit under it with his eyes closed. He says he can feel the spirit of Houdini there, pouring into him.

Sam is a little weird.

Here's how the Metamorphosis trick was supposed to go: I would handcuff Sam, and he'd get into a huge potato sack. I'd tie off the top of the sack, and then help him into the trunk. Then I'd rope and lock the trunk from the outside.

After that, we'd put up a screen (we didn't actually have the screen yet — that part would come later), and I would go behind it, and then, an instant later, Sam would appear to the audience, no longer tied up and no longer in the potato sack.

And then, when he moved the screen, *I* would be inside the potato sack, inside the trunk, handcuffed, and the trunk would still be locked and roped shut.

I suppose you'd like to know how it's done.

But if I told you, it wouldn't be magic anymore.

Sam had already mastered his part of Metamorphosis. He'd mastered some of Houdini's other tricks, too, such as picking locks, either with a pick or with the escape artist's best friend in a pinch, the bobby pin. He'd taught me how to pick a lock, too. I could even pick a lot of built-in combination locks like a pro.

The one thing I couldn't do was to get inside the trunk and have it locked down on me. It petrified me. Just the thought made me feel as if I couldn't breathe.

Right then I took a deep breath, just to make sure I still could. When I get really nervous, I think about breathing. The weird thing is, though, when you think about breathing, you realize that if you stop doing it, you die.

Which only makes you think about it even more.

It's possible that I'm just as weird as Sam.

Sam opened the trunk and took out the handcuffs and ropes.

I inhaled. "I have to study for the math test and so do you." I exhaled.

"The Great Samdini does not study for math tests," Sam bellowed in his Great Samdini voice. He handed me the ropes. "Tie the top of the sack tighter than last time, Deed. And make sure you lock the lock. Last time you —"

"Sam! I have to study. Not everyone is a genius like you, you know."

He stared at me. "You're still scared to get into the trunk, aren't you?"

"So?"

"So we can't do the trick until you get into the trunk," Sam said, exasperated. "The trick *depends* on it."

I folded my arms. "You're the one who wants to be Houdini, not me."

"And you're the one who wants to stop being scared all the time."

I turned to my dresser and looked at my pale, skinny face in the mirror. The face staring back didn't fill me with confidence. "Wanting to do something and actually being able to do it are two different things, you know."

"Agreed," Sam said. "But I, the Great Samdini, can tell you how."

I gave him my best I-doubt-it look. "How, Sam?"

"You have to want it more than you want anything in the world. And, most important of all, Deed, you have to believe in yourself."

"Puh-leeze." Irritation crept up the back of my neck. "That's what David always says. That's what *everyone* always says."

"The Great Samdini is not everyone."

I watched his reflection in the mirror as he put on the handcuffs and shimmied into the potato sack. Then he kind of fell over into the trunk. "Fasten the cuffs on me. We'll tie the sack later. I'm going to show you again that the trunk isn't scary. Think of it as a cozy little bed."

"More like a cozy little coffin." I went to him and fastened the handcuffs around his wrists. "Okay?"

"K-O." He curled up in a ball. "Close the trunk and put on the combination lock."

I closed the trunk, did the lock, and sat on it.

"Sometimes, Sam — don't tell this to anyone — sometimes I wish I really could metamorphose into someone else, you know? Even something else. A bird. So I could fly. That would be so awesome."

Sam, inside the trunk, didn't answer. I knew he was busy getting himself out of the handcuffs.

I brought my knees up to my chin and wrapped my arms around them. "If I have to be a person, I'd like to be someone like David, only a girl," I continued dreamily. "I'd be incredibly brave. And this great athlete. And I'd be so popular — everyone would love me."

I closed my eyes. I could almost see the new me.

"I'd be tall, too," I fantasized. "Not just kind of tall, but *tall* tall, so everyone would have to look up to me. Did you ever notice that everyone in my family except me is brave and tall? I'm like some kind of mutant who likes to go to the library instead of going hunting. Did you know I'm the only one in my family with a library card, Sam? Sam?"

No answer.

"Sam?"

No answer.

"You should have been out of there a long time ago, Sam!" I realized, my heart beating a tattoo of fear in my chest. "Can you hear me?"

All I could think of was how I couldn't breathe in the trunk. Maybe no one could breathe in the trunk. Maybe a person could suffocate in the —

"Sam!" I shrieked. "Answer me!"

But from inside the trunk, there was no answer.

2

My hands were shaking as I spun the combination lock. It didn't open.

Inside the trunk, nothing was happening.

"Sam? Answer me, Sam, I can't get this lock open!"

I fumbled with it some more, my hands shaking. "Sam? Oh my God, Sam!"

Frantically I worked on the lock, spinning the combination again. Sweat dripped down my face. After what felt like forever, I got the lock apart, and pushed the lid of the trunk open.

Sam sat up, a stupid grin on his face. "Miss me?"

"You jerk!" I punched him in the arm as hard as I could. "You really, really scared me!"

"You care!" Sam cried comically, throwing his arms wide. "That is so —"

"Just what do you think you're doing?"

My father, in his police uniform, loomed in the doorway. His voice was so angry that I felt ashamed, as if we were doing something horrible, even though we weren't.

"J-Just fooling around," I said nervously.

"Dee Dee, didn't your mother leave you a chores list on the bulletin board?"

I nodded.

"You haven't done any of it, have you?"

"N-No, sir," I admitted.

My mom is a nurse. Even though it was Sunday, she was working a double shift at the hospital. She worked a lot of double shifts now, because we needed the money. But I'll get to the money part later.

It used to be that we'd go to church and then out for a family lunch on Sunday. Everything was so much better back then. We used to be happy. My father hadn't *liked* me, exactly, not the way he liked my brothers, but at least he wasn't mean to me. Even when the bad thing happened with my grandmother, my father hadn't taken it out on me. But then the accident happened, two months later, and that accident changed everything.

For a long time, my father had dreamed of becoming a police captain. He loved being a cop. Everyone said he was a good one because he was fair, and he really cared about helping people. Finally, the time came for him to take the test for his promotion. Everyone was so sure he'd get it that his friends at the precinct were already planning a party for him. Only he didn't get it. Another cop, a black cop named Charles Jordan, got it instead. My dad and Mr. Jordan got the exact same score on the test and my dad had seniority, so he couldn't figure out why he had lost out.

Charles Jordan is bilingual, he was told. He speaks Spanish, and you don't.

Since when does speaking Spanish matter in Appleton, Wisconsin? My father wanted to know. Did Jordan get the job because he's black? He wanted to know.

The police chief told my father it wasn't a racial thing. Appleton was changing, he said. There was a Spanish-speaking community now and a Spanish-speaking police captain would be an asset to the city. He told my dad he could try again in two years for a promotion. I bet he clapped him on the back when he said it. Adults do that when they tell you something that is going to break your heart.

My father's heart was broken, I think. Not that he acted that way. How he acted was mad. And humiliated, I suppose, since his friends had already been planning that party and everything.

I guess it was because he was so mad that the accident happened. He must not have been watching where he was walking when he stormed out of the precinct house. It had been raining, and the steps were slick. But my dad is such a great athlete — how could that have accounted for what happened? I've pictured it in my mind so many times, even though I wasn't there. His feet must have flown out from under him. He must have been so surprised in that instant when he went tumbling down the stairs at the front of the precinct house, and landed on his back.

He couldn't get up. He was in the hospital for ten days.

Thank God, Mom said, when Dad came home, that he wasn't paralyzed.

But Dad wasn't thanking anyone. He had to wear a back brace. The doctors couldn't decide if he should have surgery or not.

Now he couldn't go bowling or hunting or do any of the things he loved to do. His new superior officer, Charles Jordan, the man who had gotten the promotion instead of my father, had to put him on desk duty, because he wasn't able to do anything else.

And he might never be able to again.

The doctors made that decision, not Mr. Jordan. But to my father, it was Charles Jordan's fault.

My father was in pain all the time. He had pills for the pain, but refused to take them. He thought it was a sign of weakness, is how Mom explained it to me. So when the pain got really bad, he would yell at me.

It was after the accident that my father started saying bad things about black people. But it was just so weird. I had never heard my father say things like that before. It was like some other per-

17

son's words — nasty, cold, full of hate — were coming out of my father's mouth.

My father also refused to go back to church. He said he didn't want people pitying him. Mom said she wouldn't go without him, and besides, she'd make more money if she worked a double shift on Sundays, and we certainly could use the money.

It always made Dad's face tight when she said that.

Just like it was tight now.

"What is wrong with you, Dee Dee?" my father snapped.

"N-Nothing," I said, my voice small.

Dad looked at Sam, sitting in the trunk, with just his head poking out of the potato sack. "Dee Dee has a lot of chores to do, Sam. It's time for you to go home."

"Actually, my father made soy loaf for lunch," Sam said. "I choose chores."

My father gave me a hard look. "I have to go back to the station house. I expect all your chores to be done before I get home tonight, young lady."

"Y-Yes, sir," I stammered.

He shook his head at me. He did that a lot. Then he turned around and left. I heard the front door bang.

Silently, Sam got out of the potato sack and out of the trunk. He didn't even protest when I started pushing the trunk back into my closet. All the fun was gone.

It didn't used to be like that. We used to all have fun. But not anymore. And there was never enough money.

Worst of all, my father hated me. And I didn't know why.

Sam and I trudged into the kitchen. My dad was right, it was a mess. I took the milk out of the refrigerator and drank some from the carton, then I handed it to Sam.

"Here first or there first?" I asked him.

He downed the last of the milk. "There," he decided, wiping off his milk mustache. He threw the carton across the room into the trash. "Might as well get it over with."

Sam knew that every Sunday I had "here" chores, meaning what I had to do at home, and one big "there" chore. The "there" chore was worse than putting up with my obnoxious little brother, Andy, or cleaning and mopping the kitchen, or even scrubbing the toilets.

The "there" chore was the most dreaded chore of all.

It was #6 on Mom's Sunday list.

I had to get on my bike, ride two miles, and go inside an ugly brick building that smelled like death.

And then I had to do the scariest thing.

I had to visit the vegetable that used to be my grandmother.

3

I balanced Sam on my handlebars and biked the two miles to the Happy Appleton Acres Home for Assisted Living.

"When are you going to get your own bike, Sam?" I puffed, as I practically stood on the pedals to go up the final hill.

"The Great Samdini would look like a dork riding his own bike."

"So what do you look like riding on my handlebars?"

His long brown hair flapped in the breeze. "Like you're my chauffeur, of course."

I turned the bike into the parking lot.

"Happy Appleton Acres," Sam said, hopping off my handlebars. He looked at the building. "Someone with a twisted sense of humor must have named this place. No one in there is happy, and there are no acres. Unless you count the acres of old people, vegging out."

I locked my bike up and we walked into the

building. It's modern and clean, with nice murals on the walls and nice maroon carpeting that matched the nice maroon chairs in the nice hallway.

My parents insist that it doesn't smell in there, but it does.

I breathed through my mouth. "I hate it here."

"Ditto."

"Then why do you come with me every Sunday?"

Sam shrugged and stuck his hands in his pockets.

We walked past the reception desk, and waved to Mrs. B., the nice fat lady who worked behind the desk.

"She looks well today!" Mrs. B. exclaimed, waving back to us with her turkey-wattle arm.

"Okay, what's the bet?" I asked Sam.

He thought for a minute. "I say she won't."

"I say she will. For a buck. Okay?"

He nodded. "K-O. You got yourself a bet."

We rounded the corner.

There, in the hallway, sat a shriveled-up, white-haired old lady in a wheelchair, with her young aide nearby.

The old lady's eyes focused on me. "Laurie? Is that Laurie?"

"No, Mrs. Elder, that's Mrs. Deeton's granddaughter, same as every Sunday," her aide said wearily.

The old lady's eyes burned with fury. "Laurie! You stole my husband, you hussy!" She shook her fist at me.

Sam and I hurried around the next corner, falling all over each other, laughing.

I held out my hand. "Pay up."

Sam's jaw fell open. "You didn't win."

"Did too. She thought I was Laurie and she cursed at me, now pay up."

"Deed, she always thinks you're Laurie. And 'hussy' isn't a curse word."

"It is in my house."

We came to a stop in front of a maroon-colored door, number 104, with a name plate on it.

MRS. DEANNA DEETON, it read.

I looked at Sam for moral support. He pretended to slit his wrists.

I opened the door.

There she was, lying in bed, facing the ceiling, stuck in a body that couldn't move with a mouth that couldn't speak and eyes that couldn't see.

That's how she'd been for almost a year now, when she'd gone downhill after a stroke. My mom had told me that a stroke happened when a person's brain didn't get enough blood. Some people got better after strokes, and some people didn't.

My grandmother — Meemaw, we always called her — didn't. She got worse.

The truth was, I didn't miss her all that much. She hadn't been one of those grandmothers that

22

lavished love and attention on you, like Sam's Grandma Bette. And she certainly hasn't been very nice to my father, who was her only kid. I guess she wanted him to be more like her, someone who liked books and plays and ideas, instead of someone who liked motorcycles and hiking and sports.

Come to think of it, she treated Dad the same way Dad treated me.

Huh.

Meemaw had claimed she was a writer, but I never saw anything that she wrote. When Grampa Bill died, she sold their little house, took his life insurance money, and went on a first-class trip around the world.

She didn't come back to Appleton for three years.

When she did come back, she had no home and hardly any money. Dad asked her how she planned to live. She told him that a writer could always make a living, but until she sold something she'd accept his assistance.

One day, right after I turned ten, she summoned me to meet her for lunch at the hotel where she was temporarily staying. To give me my inheritance, she said.

I was so excited. I didn't know she was poor, so I thought maybe she was about to give me a lot of money. Or a computer! I was desperate for a computer.

Mom drove me and dropped me off. After Meemaw and I ate some terrible food in the hotel restaurant, she said it was time to give me my inheritance.

Money? For a computer? I held my breath.

She reached into her purse. And took out a neatly typed list, which she handed to me.

It was a list of one hundred books — the hundred best books ever written for young people. Everything I needed to know about life and growing up was in those books, Meemaw told me. And while some people might not agree that all of those books were suitable for a young person, she, Meemaw, knew better. After I read each one, I was to report to her, and then, she said, we would discuss them together.

She sat there, waiting, like I should *thank* her.

I was so mad when I got home that I threw the stupid book list away. But David fished it out of the trash and tacked it up on my bulletin board.

Well fine, it could hang there forever for all I cared. What a dumb, useless inheritance. I could find books on my own. What I needed was a *computer*.

That was the last time I had a conversation with her. A few days later, she had the stroke. And ever since then, all the money my parents made went to Happy Appleton Acres, to take care of Meemaw. I never knew a nursing home was so expensive, but it costs a fortune. I couldn't get a computer, and we never had any money, all because of her.

For the first year or so, when Meemaw could still feed herself, get to the bathroom, and understand what we were saying to her, I didn't mind so much. She couldn't talk or write, but at least she still communicated with us, by blinking. Once for yes, twice for no.

Then she got worse. She had a feeding tube down her throat, an IV in her arm, and she wore diapers that someone had to change. She had stopped blinking a long time ago. Finally we all just stopped talking to her. All she did was lay there. She couldn't even see.

It cost even more money to take care of her, because she needed special care. Money my parents didn't have. Since Dad was probably never going to get a promotion on account of his injury, money we probably never *would* have.

And Meemaw wasn't even *in there* to appreciate it.

My father still visited her twice a week. He would just sit there, gazing out the window, not saying a word.

Every Sunday, he forced me to go.

Sam and I sat down, and he pulled out his deck of playing cards so he could work on card tricks. It's what we did every Sunday. After an hour of card tricks, we'd leave.

"Nothing up my sleeves," Sam said, shoving the sleeves of his T-shirt up his right arm, then his left. He held the cards in his right hand, between his thumb and middle finger. He was supposed to make the entire deck fly into his left hand. But something went wrong, and the cards flew onto the bed, all over my grandmother.

Gingerly, we picked them off of her. She didn't move.

Sam stared down at her from one side of the bed, me from the other. "You think she's in there, Deed?"

"Nope," I said. "If she was in there, she'd still be blinking."

My eyes slid to the photograph of my grandmother that hung over her bed. She was very young, smiling. She didn't look anything like the paralyzed, blind, speechless woman in the bed. But that wasn't what was so terrible about it.

What was so terrible was, that photograph looked just like me.

I tore my eyes away from the picture. "Come on, Sam, do the trick again, you wrecked it that time." We sat down.

"Nothing up my sleeves," Sam began.

Just then the door opened, and in walked David. "Hey, guys, what's up?" he said easily.

I was surprised to see him. "What're you doing here?"

"The same thing you're doing." He went to Meemaw's bed and kissed her papery skin.

I never kissed her. I shuddered as his lips brushed against her cheek. "But you were here this morning."

My parents didn't make David come see Meemaw, he just did it. Since we'd stopped going to church, I knew he'd been spending Sunday mornings at the nursing home.

"Nope, I got busy," David said. He pulled a chair up to her bed and took her hand. "So, Meemaw, how's it going today? It's really sunny out, more like summer than fall. Want me to open the window for you?"

He waited, as if she were actually going to answer him.

"I'll just do it, then," he told her. "You'll like the fresh air."

He went to the window and opened it wide.

"There." He sat back down and took her hand again. "Hey, remember that test I told you about, on *Hamlet*? I got a B. Pretty good, huh? Okay, I admit it, I read the *Cliff Notes* or I never would have understood it. What was it you used to say? '*Cliff Notes* never taught anyone to think, David.' Did I get it right, Meemaw?"

He grinned and looked at her expectantly.

"Why are you *doing* that?" I blurted out.

"Doing what?" David asked me.

27

"Talking to her like you're having a conversation!"

David shrugged. "Because we are."

"You are not," I said. "*You're* talking. *She* isn't."

"She does a lot of listening these days."

I narrowed my eyes at him. "No one else talks to her, you know."

He nodded. "Yeah. She doesn't like that."

I gave him a withering look. "How do you know? Did she *tell* you?"

"No. But she follows everything I say."

"Does not," I insisted. "If she did, she'd blink."

"Maybe she doesn't want to blink."

"Maybe her mind is Swiss cheese," Sam offered.

David rubbed his chin thoughtfully. "I've been thinking about why she doesn't blink anymore. See, she can't read or write or even talk. Those are all the things she loved to do, right? So the reason she quit blinking is because she's too mad."

I gave him a dubious look.

"You know, frustrated," David explained. "I mean, think about it, Darce. Picture yourself in her situation. Wouldn't you be mad?"

Picture yourself in her situation. My eyes returned to that photo of young Meemaw over her bed. It was like looking at a photograph of myself. I shuddered again.

"The way I figure it," David continued, "one day she'll want me to know something so bad that she can't help herself. And then . . . then, she'll blink again."

"Hey, did you guys know that Houdini tried to communicate with the dead?" Sam suddenly asked.

"What does that have to do with anything?" I asked him, irritated.

Sam shrugged. "Well, if your grandmother was dead, we might have an easier time of it."

I stared at him. "You know, your brain doesn't work like anyone else's."

Sam nodded. "Thank you."

"Could Houdini do it? Did it work?" David asked him.

"No," Sam admitted. "But every time I sit under the Metamorphosis statue, I can feel him talking to me." I rolled my eyes.

David took Meemaw's hand. "Sometimes when I'm really quiet, I can feel Meemaw talking to me, too. I can't explain it. And I sure can't prove it. So I just . . . I just believe it. I guess I just accept it on faith."

I folded my arms skeptically. "Definition, please."

"Faith," Sam began. "Noun. A —"

"Not *you*," I told him, my voice withering. I looked at my brother.

He puffed some air through his pursed lips and scrunched up his forehead. Like Dad, words were not his strong suit. "Let's see. Faith is . . . it's when your heart tells you something is true, even if you can't prove it. Haven't you ever felt that way?"

"No," I said bluntly, kicking my sneaker into the carpet. "It's not like she was such a wonderful grandmother. All she ever gave me was a stupid book list."

"What number are you on now?" David asked.

"Twenty-seven," I confessed. "*A Tree Grows in Brooklyn.*"

"Is it good?"

"Beyond," I admitted.

No one said anything. The room was so quiet. I closed my eyes and tried to be like David, to hear my grandmother talking to me inside my head. I *wanted* to hear what David heard, so I could say to him: "Wow, it's a miracle! Only us two in the entire world can hear Meemaw in our heads!"

But I didn't hear Meemaw.

All I heard was a big nothing.

When I opened my eyes, Sam had slid down the wall and was deeply involved in a card trick, and David was talking quietly to Meemaw again.

I thought about that book list she'd given me two years ago, still pinned up on the bulletin board in my room, the corners curled and yellowing now, twenty-seven titles neatly checked off. *To Kill a Mockingbird. Charlotte's Web. The Little Prince.*

She was right about one thing. So far every single book on that list was great. But she had been wrong about something else.

We were never going to get to discuss them.

"So, the reason I wasn't here this morning, Meemaw," David was saying, "is because I was with her."

Huh? What had I just missed?

"I really want you to meet her. You'll like her, she's smart — a whole lot smarter than me. She got an A on that *Hamlet* test without *Cliff Notes*. Her family just moved here, and from the very first day we met, it was like —"

"Uh, excuse me," I interrupted. "*Who* just moved here?"

"Darce, something so amazing has happened to me. It's like — my life was going along, and then, like, in an instant, because of one person, everything changed."

"Changed like how?" I asked suspiciously.

He walked over to the window and stared out. "It's like . . . like you don't even realize there's this hole in your life, until this person comes along and fills it."

"You, light up my life . . ." Sam sang dramatically and off-key.

"Some girl?" I asked David. "You met some girl or something?"

"You give me hope . . . to carry on . . ." Sam warbled.

David turned around. His eyes were shining. "Not just some girl, Darce. *The* girl."

"You light up my days . . ."

"Shut up!" I turned to David. "What does that mean, *the* girl?"

"It means . . . man, I'm so excited I can't even say this right." He sat back down with Meemaw and took her hand again. "I wanted to ask you, can I bring her here to meet you?"

He waited. Meemaw didn't blink.

"I know you mean yes, Meemaw," he said softly.

David walked to the door and opened it, and held out his hand to someone in the hall.

From where I stood, all I could see was a small hand taking his, a slender arm. A girl. *The* girl. Coming into the room. Hand-in-hand. With *my* brother.

She was slender and tall, with long, dark hair and a sweetly smiling face.

David put his arm around her.

"Meemaw, Darce, Sam, I want you to meet Jayne Evans," David said. "This is the girl I love."

4

"**S**o, in conclusion, Princess Diana was beautiful but she was nice, too. She did many things to help people, such as getting rid of land mines. Also her clothes were beautiful and cost a lot of money and she gave them to charity after she wore them. This is why Princess Diana is the person I admire most."

Amanda Bliss finished her speech and smiled at Mrs. Pritcher. Amanda looks like one of those child models in the *American Girl* catalog. Plus she was already getting a figure. She also had the brains and personality of dental floss, if dental floss was mean.

"Thank you, Amanda. Good job!" Mrs. Pritcher wrote something in her grade book.

I looked over at Sam, who pretended to shoot himself in the head. He felt the same way about Amanda that I did.

Last year, we did this unit on Martin Luther King, Jr., called "I Have a Dream." We all had to write a paper on our own dream. Amanda wrote that her dream was to turn the letters on a TV game show. Our teacher loved it. She framed it for the bulletin board.

Sam leaned over to me. "What do you want to bet she gets an A. And my parents wonder why I hate school."

I barely heard him, because my mind wasn't on Amanda. It was on something else.

Or should I say, some*one* else.

JAYNE EVANS SMELLS, I wrote on a sheet of notebook paper in big block letters. I crossed out smells. STINKS, I wrote instead. That was better. JAYNE EVANS STINKS LIKE —

"Dee Dee Deeton?"

Caught! My hand flew over my scribbles, my face burned, as if Mrs. Pritcher had read what I'd written.

"Yes, M-Mrs. P-Pritcher?"

Henry Farmer, the biggest, meanest kid in our class, snorted out a laugh, and pretended to stutter. Amanda Bliss giggled and put her hand over her mouth. Sam shot a rubber band at Henry.

"That is more than enough," Mrs. Pritcher said sharply. She turned to me. "Would you please read your speech to the class, Dee Dee?"

For three days I had sat there while Mrs. Pritcher called on other kids to read their speeches. Sam had read his the day before, but I had yet to read mine. As each day passed, the stupid speech I had written about David made me madder and madder. Because my wonderful brother had turned into a traitor, who was in love with stinky Jayne.

"Dee Dee?" Mrs. Pritcher said. "We're waiting."

I looked up at the clock. Only six minutes of school left. I had almost, but not quite, escaped.

I stood up on shaky legs and made the long walk from my seat in the back of the classroom. Everyone was staring at me. I looked down at my speech.

JAYNE EVANS STINKS LIKE was what I read.

In my nervousness, I had grabbed the paper on which I'd been scribbling, instead of grabbing my speech.

"Go ahead, Dee Dee," Mrs. Pritcher prompted me.

Breathe in, breathe out. Should I explain that I'd picked up the wrong paper, and walk all the way back to my seat? What if I tripped? Or stuttered? What if I tripped and *then* I stuttered? I stood there breathing, frozen.

Every second that passed felt like an hour.

"In this l-l-lifetime, D-D-Deeton," Henry Farmer said, mimicking my stutter. A few kids tittered.

"Henry, any more of that and you're in Mr. Clarentini's office," Mrs. Pritcher warned him. "Go ahead, Dee Dee."

I will not stutter, I will not stutter, I will not stutter, I told myself. I forced myself to slow down and breathe deeply, the way the speech therapist had showed me.

"'The Person I Admire Most,' by Dee Dee Dee-ton," I mumbled slowly, pretending to read from my paper, which was blank except for JAYNE EVANS STINKS LIKE.

I took a deep breath. I let it out again.

"The person I admire most is my f-father," I invented, staring hard at that paper. "He is a p-policeman. He's b-brave. Once he got a special medal for bravery," I continued, making it up as I went along. "This summer he took our family to Florida on vacation. We went deep-sea fishing in the Gulf of Mexico. My dad caught the biggest fish and made us eat it. This is why he is the person I admire most."

Silence. Someone snickered. Finally, I looked up. Sam was pretending to hang himself with an invisible rope.

"Is that it?" Mrs. Pritcher asked me.

I nodded.

"It's quite short," she noted.

I nodded again.

"Well, thank you, Dee Dee." She scribbled something in her grade book. I had a feeling it was a big, fat D.

"Now let's hear from —"

Saved by the bell.

Kids flew from the classroom like they'd been

shot from a cannon. I went back to my desk and started to shove my stuff into my backpack.

Sam sat on my desk, looking at me incredulously. "'My dad caught the biggest fish and made us *eat* it?'" he quoted. "'This is why he is the person I admire *most*?'"

I shrugged and looped my backpack over my shoulders. We headed for the door.

"Correct me if I'm wrong," Sam said. "I seem to recall this excellent speech you wrote about your brother."

"I took the wrong paper up there with me," I told him, as we dodged around a kid on in-line skates being chased by a screaming teacher.

"So? All you had to do was go back to your seat and get the right paper."

"Well, maybe I didn't want to do that. Anyway, maybe the speech I wrote stunk."

"And maybe it was great, the best one in the whole class," Sam said. "The one you gave, now *that* stunk."

Just at that moment, Henry Farmer bumped into Sam, hard. "Watch it, Shrimp-boy!" He loomed over Sam like a truck looking down at a tinker toy. Amanda Bliss, who I had heard was going steady with Henry, just stood there, grinning at her hero.

Sam stopped in his tracks. Of all the insults he endured, this was his most hated.

"You shouldn't have said that," Sam said into Henry's belt buckle.

"Yeah?" Henry jeered. "Whatja gonna do about it?"

"D-Don't do anything," I warned Sam. "Count to ten."

In fourth grade he had gotten his nose broken when he'd kicked Henry Farmer for calling him that exact same name.

"Intelligent people don't settle things with violence," his father had told him, and grounded him for a month.

Henry belly-butted Sam. "Got something to say, Shrimp-boy?"

Sam stood there, gritting his teeth. "I've decided to let you go this time," he finally said. "Just don't let it happen again."

"I'm so sure," Amanda snorted, flicking her hair over her shoulder like in a shampoo commercial.

Henry pushed Sam again, then he ran off with Amanda, both of them laughing like the idiots they were.

"You did the right thing," I assured Sam.

"Wrong," he said. His eyes wouldn't meet mine. "In the middle school jungle, height plus might equals right."

We walked outside into the bright afternoon sunshine. Sam put on his round sunglasses. He thinks they make him look older.

"Bus or bike?" I asked him.

"Need you ask?"

We headed for the bike rack near the parking lot.

"So, want to know what I think?" Sam asked me.

"No." I unlocked my bike and got on. Sam climbed on my handlebars and I pedaled out of the parking lot.

"Hey, Weenie Samdini!" Henry Farmer called, as he waited to get on the school bus Sam would have been taking. "Why don't you do a magic trick and make yourself grow so you can k-k-kiss Stutter-girl?"

"It's frightening to think that one day his vote will count as much as yours or mine," Sam mused.

I pedaled east, away from school.

"So, as I was saying," Sam said, half turning his head so I could hear him, "I think the reason you didn't give the speech you wrote about David is that you're so angry at him for falling for Jayne."

"I told you! I took the wrong paper up with me, that's all." I made a left on College Street, which leads to Houdini Plaza in Appleton Center.

"Wrong-a-mundo," Sam insisted smugly. "The Great Samdini knows all and sees all."

"The Great Samdini is really irritating me."

As I biked past the Metamorphosis sculpture, it

39

reminded me of what had happened with Jayne the night before, and I got even more irritated.

"She is just so full of it," I fumed.

"I take it we're talking about your beloved Jayne."

"Ha. Last night, when David brought her over, and you told her about our Metamorphosis trick, she pretended to get all excited about it, right?"

"Possibly she really *was* excited."

"Possibly she's a big hypocrite who *pretended* to get excited so that David would like her more."

"Possibly," Sam allowed. "It worked."

I pedaled around the corner. "Have you noticed how weird David has gotten? All he cares about is *her*. I don't even exist. You know how he always lets me hang out with him after his football games. But this Friday he's got a date after the game with *her*. And he can't help me make my papier-mâché volcano for the science fair, even though he promised. He has to study with *her*."

"You can say her name, you know," Sam said.

"No, I can't. Her name is a curse. So from now on, I'm just calling her the J-word."

Sam nodded. "Catchy."

"I am so onto her. Like how she says 'Oh, Davie, let's take Dee Dee with us!'" I mimicked her voice. "She doesn't really want me to come with them. It's just a pathetic ploy to get *Davie* to like her."

"Worse than pathetic," Sam said dramatically.

"You remember that old sci-fi flick we watched on TV, *Invasion of the Body Snatchers*? I think Jayne has invaded David's mind, leaving behind nothing but a hideous, empty, zombie shell."

"Very funny." I turned my bike up Sam's driveway and hopped off.

"You wanna come in? Bette's over. She baked."

Bette was Sam's grandmother. She asks everyone to call her by her first name.

I rewrapped my scrunchie around my limp ponytail. "It's Wednesday. You have Hebrew."

Sam had to go to his Hebrew tutor's house twice a week to prepare for his *bar mitzvah*. It's a Jewish ceremony that would officially make him an adult.

Sam hated his Hebrew tutor. Besides, he felt he could teach himself on the computer better than any tutor ever could.

"If I flush lots of water in my eye it'll get red and pass for pinkeye and I can call in sick. Just a sec."

"Nah." I straddled my bike. "Hey, my birthday dinner Sunday is at six, okay?"

"K-O," Sam agreed.

I pushed some stray hairs behind my ear. "You don't think David would miss my birthday so he could be with the J-word, do you?"

Sam stiffened his arms and legs, and walked like Frankenstein. "Who knows? He's an android zombie now, his mind completely controlled by —"

"You're a total dork, Sam!" I yelled over my shoulder as I pedaled down his driveway.

I turned toward my house and was surprised to see David's beat-up bomb of a car in the driveway. Over the summer, he'd worked at the Video Shack after school, which was how he'd paid for his car. He still worked there on some afternoons.

I hurried into the house, so glad that he was home. Ever since last Sunday, when he'd forced the J-word on me, he'd spent all his time either with her or talking about her. Maybe I could read him the new story I was writing, I thought, as I pushed open the front door. Or we could —

Frantic scrambling on the living room couch. Two bodies.

David's.

And *hers*.

They had been lying there. Kissing. All their clothes were on.

But *still*.

I marched right past them, straight for my room.

"Darce! Hey, Darce! Aren't you home kinda early?" David's voice was breathless and embarrassed.

"Go get her, Davie," I heard the J-word say. "You know how much she loves you."

I marched into my room and slammed the door as hard as I could.

Bam.

I only wished I was slamming it on the J-word's head.

No place was safe from her. No *one* was safe from her.

Suddenly, it was all clear to me. I knew what I had to do. For David's own good, I had to figure out a way to break them up.

5

Sunday afternoon. My birthday.
    I was officially twelve years old.

I stared at my face in the mirror over my dresser. I didn't look any different. I was just as short and skinny and flat as always. I stuck my fists under my T-shirt to see how it would look if something was under there.

The J-word definitely had something under there.

I studied my profile.

Maybe if I introduced David to another girl, a nicer, smarter, prettier girl, he'd dump the J-word. He wouldn't exactly love this other girl, they'd just hang out, like David had with all his girlfriends in the past. And then everything would be how it used to be. Before *her*.

"Ha! What are you doing — as if I didn't know!" my little brother, Andy, hooted from the doorway.

My face burned with humiliation. I took my fists

out from under my T-shirt. "Shut up and get out of my room."

"I'm not *in* your room," he pointed out smugly, his feet firmly planted in the hallway. "I'm supposed to tell you that dinner's almost ready but you're not supposed to go in the kitchen."

Because I felt so ornery I headed straight for the kitchen. I could smell the cake my mom had baked, double chocolate chip with chocolate frosting, my favorite.

"Wrap Dee Dee's present while I frost the cake," I heard my mom say.

I stopped. I couldn't very well go in.

"We got another late notice on the car loan," she told Dad. "And the bill for Appleton Acres is overdue. And if we don't send something to Visa —"

"I know all about the bills, Claire," my father said in that new, tight voice of his.

"I can ask for more overtime —"

"Do you really think that's what I want?"

Silence.

My dad: "I'm not wrapping this very well."

"You're doing fine," Mom said.

"A sweater," Dad muttered. "She wanted a computer. She *deserves* a computer."

"Maybe next year," Mom said.

"If I had gotten that promotion —" Dad began. Then he swore.

This was shocking. No one ever, *ever* was allowed to curse in our house.

45

"Don't you think I lie in bed every night, thinking about what that black so-and-so did to our life?" my father exploded. "I *needed* that promotion. I *earned* it."

"Charles scored the same as you did, Doug," my mom said. "And he speaks Spanish —"

"Whose side are you on?"

"I'm just saying you can't blame this on race."

My mother sounded so tired. It hurt my heart.

"Bull," my father snapped. "There's only one reason that Jordan is captain, telling me what to do, making the money I *should* be making, while I'm chained to some dead-end desk job with a messed-up back. And that one reason is the color of his skin."

"You never used to say things like that," Mom said sadly. "It used to make you so mad, cops who talked the way you're talking now. You said you'd never be like them."

"Yeah, well, I was an idiot."

"No," Mom said. "You were my hero."

I got a funny feeling inside. In our memory box, in the attic, was my parents' yearbook from Appleton West High School. They had been voted Cutest Couple. Under Mom's name it said "wants to be a nurse and a mother." Under Dad's name it said "wants to be a cop and help make the world safe."

Mom was voted Best Smile. Dad was voted Most Heroic.

That was then. This was now.

I went out to the front porch and looked down the empty street, watching for David's car. The only person coming was Sam, walking across his lawn to ours.

"Hi," he mumbled self-consciously, in a very un-Sam-like fashion. He was dressed in a very un-Sam-like fashion, too. His hair was slicked back, and he wore a sport coat over his HOUDINI LIVES T-shirt.

"Why do you look like that?" I asked him.

"A question I've often asked myself," he replied. "Basically it's a question of genetics. If both your parents are short, then odds are you'll be short. Sadly, it's out of my hands."

"David isn't here yet."

"He'll be here."

"How do you know?"

"Deed, he's never missed your birthday."

"That was before the J-word."

Sam leaned against a pillar. "He's allowed to have a girlfriend, you know."

"Big duh, Sam."

He shoved his hands deep into his pockets. "'Cuz, you know, eventually you'll have a boy-friend."

"Yuh, about as soon as you'll have a girlfriend," I snorted sarcastically. I looked down the street again.

"Yuh," Sam agreed. "That's what I was thinking."

"You're acting really weird, Sam."

My mother came out on the porch. Lately there were dark circles under her eyes and two grooves, like quote marks, on her forehead. Every time she and my dad argued, they got deeper. At that moment, it looked like a river could run through there.

She put her arm around my shoulders. "I can't believe my little girl is twelve. You're almost a teenager." She kissed the top of my head. "Ready to eat, sweetie?"

"David isn't home yet."

"You want to wait?"

"Of *course* I want to wait."

Andy burst out onto the porch. "Mom, I'm starving."

"Dee Dee wants to wait for David. It's her birthday."

"David knows enough to be on time," my father said irritably as he, too, came outside. He grimaced noticeably as he stepped onto the porch.

"Do you want a Darvocet?" Mom asked him, her voice low.

"If I wanted a Darvocet, I would have taken one."

He used his pain voice — the one that meant his back was killing him. I had gotten to know it really well. Sometimes I wanted to yell at him, "Take a stupid pill! It won't mean that you're a bad person!"

"I hate to see you in so much pain, Doug," Mom said.

Dad reached out and touched Mom's hand. He wasn't much with words, but she knew what he meant, and she smiled at him, even though her eyes were still sad.

Sam's parents' car pulled into their driveway. When they got out, they waved over to us.

Mom waved back. Dad didn't.

Sam's parents are both lawyers. My father wasn't fond of lawyers. Too many times, he said, good cops make good arrests, only to have lawyers find a way to get the bad guys off.

"David's probably with *her*," I muttered under my breath, willing my brother's car to come down the street.

"Jayne's a nice girl," my mom said. She gave my father a loving look. "You and I fell in love in high school."

"Yuck," Andy said. "I'm not getting in love until I'm, like, thirty or something."

"You never know," my father teased. I could tell he was trying to be nice. "Sometimes you end up marrying your high school sweetheart."

Marrying? Could that happen with David and the J-word?

I shivered. The evenings were getting colder. Soon the leaves would change, then die. Next door, Sam's parents were laughing about something as they went into the house.

"Dad, I mean it, I'm gonna faint or something I'm so hungry," Andy whined.

"You could chew on your own arm," Sam suggested. "It's organic."

Dad headed in. "We're sitting down to eat."

"But we can't!" I protested. "David isn't —"

At that moment, David's clunky, old car turned into our street.

"He's here!" I cried, running down the driveway to meet him.

"I was so afraid you forgot." When he got out I threw my arms around his neck.

He swung me in a circle. "Are you kidding? Turning twelve is big stuff."

That's when the brilliant idea hit me. If I acted as adult and sophisticated as you-know-who, David would want to hang out with me again. And that would buy me some time until I could introduce him to someone much better than you-know-who.

He reached into the car, bringing out a huge, gift-wrapped box.

The day before, when I had been merely eleven, I'd have grabbed it, and jumped up and down with excitement. Now I just smiled, the way I had seen the J-word smile.

"Is that for me?"

"You betcha, birthday girl."

"You're late, son," Dad called mildly.

"Sorry, Dad. I got held up."

We all went into the dining room, where David

added his present to the small pile on the side table, and we all sat down to eat.

Mom brought out all my favorites — homemade pizza with extra cheese, nachos smothered in chili, and Buffalo wings with her secret recipe hot sauce.

"Well, Davie, how was your day?" I asked him, smoothing my napkin on my lap.

"*Davie*?" Andy echoed, making a face.

I ignored him, and nibbled daintily on a chicken wing.

"Great," David replied. "I saw Meemaw this morning. I thought her color looked better."

"Good for you, son," my father said.

"Yes," I agreed. "It's so sweet that Davie visits Meemaw. But then, that's just the kind of person Davie is."

"What's her problem?" Andy asked.

"*Body Snatchers*," Sam replied knowingly.

I cut my eyes at him. "You're *so* amusing."

He pretended to choke himself to death.

We all ate and talked and laughed like we hadn't in a long time. David didn't mention the J-word once. And my father was actually nice to me.

"Watch out, Dee Dee," Dad teased, "one of these days you're gonna turn into a looker, just like your mom."

"I'm so sure," I snorted, embarrassed. After all, I didn't look *anything* like my mom, as far as I could see. I knew who I looked like. She was laying in a bed at Appleton Acres that very minute, drooling.

"You'll see, Dee Dee," Mom said. "Your time is coming."

"In what century?" Andy asked, as he blew bubbles into his milk.

"That's enough," my father told him. He reached over carefully, so as not to move his back, and pulled on my ponytail. For Dad, this was a sign of affection. "You're okay, Dee Dee."

Big deal. I was okay.

After dinner, Andy, Sam, and David cleared the table. Then Mom went into the kitchen to get my cake.

"Hey, get the lights out there," she called.

Sam flicked off the lights. Mom carried out my cake, alight with thirteen candles, twelve and one to grow on. Everyone sang "Happy Birthday" to me, and then I made a wish, and blew out all the candles.

"What did you wish for, Dee Dee?" Andy asked, as Mom cut the cake and passed it around.

I laughed mysteriously, the way I had heard the J-word laugh, and flicked my hair over my shoulders the way Amanda Bliss flicked hers.

"I know what she wished for," Andy said slyly. He put both fists under his T-shirt so that it stuck way out in front.

David started to laugh before he could stop himself. I felt my face blush crimson.

Andy had ruined *everything*! How could he humiliate me like that in front of everyone? And on my *birthday*!

"Idiot!" I slapped him hard on the arm.

"*You're* the idiot!" He slapped me back.

"Just shut up! I hate you!" I went to hit him again. By mistake my arm hit my glass of milk, and it went flying across the table, splattering all over my father's pale blue knit shirt.

"For crying out loud, Dee Dee!" My father jumped up, milk dripping off of him.

"I'm sorry, it was an —"

Dad gasped and grabbed his back.

"What?" Mom hurried to him.

"Spasm," Dad managed between clenched teeth.

"I'll help you to the bedroom, Dad," David said, reaching for my father's elbow. "You can lie down."

Mom hovered over him. "Should I call the doctor?"

"I don't want the doctor and I don't want to lie down!" Dad thundered. "I'm not a damn invalid."

Mom and David sat back down. Mom's face was white.

Slowly, Dad sat, too, his face pinched with pain.

"Look what you did," Andy said to me.

"*Me*? You're the one who —"

Dad banged his fist on the table so hard, the dishes jumped. "Stop it!" He pointed at me. "You

53

hit your little brother, young lady. Don't tell me you didn't."

"But it was because he —"

"I am so sick of your excuses for everything!" Dad raged. "Nothing is ever your fault. You never think of anyone but yourself."

"Hey, Dad, come on, it's Darcy's birthday," David said.

"It's always something," my father went on, his face mottled with pain and fury. "You're going to learn to toe the line around here, young lady. Do you hear me? I *said* do you hear me?"

I pushed out of my chair and ran to my bedroom, slamming the door behind me. I flung myself on my bed. My birthday was ruined.

Everything was ruined.

6

Tears ran down my cheeks. I put the pillow over my head.

There was a knock on my door.

"Go away," I said from under my pillow.

"It's me," David called softly.

I heard the door open, then felt David's weight on the bed as he sat next to me.

"Dad didn't mean that, Darce."

"Yes he did," I sniffled from under the pillow. "Why does he hate me?"

"He doesn't."

"Ha," I said from under the pillow.

"He's in a lot of pain. Losing out on the promotion. And then hurting his back."

"Well, *I* didn't do it," I said, fisting the tears off my cheek. "It's not like it's *my* fault."

"And the money thing," David went on. "Meemaw's doctor says she needs a private night nurse. That costs major bucks."

I sat up. "Well, I didn't do that, either."

"Yeah, I know." David sighed. "Dad was just counting on that promotion so much."

"Who cares about some stupid promotion? My birthday is wrecked."

David put his arm around me. "Hey, kiddo, let's not let it be wrecked, okay? You've still got all those presents waiting out there."

I didn't say anything.

"Want me to get you a tissue?"

I nodded.

He went to the bathroom and came back with tissues and a wet washcloth. I blew my nose and he wiped the washcloth across my face. "Better?"

I nodded again, and leaned my head against him.

"David?"

"What?"

"You know how Dad says Charles Jordan only got the promotion Dad wanted because he's black. Do you think that's true?"

"No, I don't."

"Do you think Dad hates black people?"

"No way," David said firmly. "He and Mom didn't raise us that way. Dad's way too fair for that."

I picked at a cuticle. "I think maybe he's changed."

"Look, Dad isn't perfect —"

"Big duh," I muttered.

"I know he takes stuff out on you, Darce. It's so weird, you know? Because Meemaw used to do the same thing to him, remember? She'd send some story she wrote to a magazine, hoping they'd publish it. But they never did. Every time she got another one of those rejection letters, she'd get mad at Dad like it was his fault."

"I never knew she wrote stories and sent them to magazines."

David shrugged. "I guess you were too young to know about it. But the thing is, even when Meemaw yelled at Dad, I always knew she loved him. Just like I know Dad loves you."

I felt an ache in my throat. "Maybe if he said the words to me, just once, I'd believe that he loved me a little. And then I could love him back."

"It'll happen, Darce."

I rolled my eyes. "You have faith, I suppose?"

"Yeah, birthday girl, I do. In you."

We went back into the dining room. Only Mom and Sam were there. Mom was sipping a cup of coffee. Sam was showing her a card trick.

"Where's Dad and Andy?" I asked.

"Andy's watching TV and your dad went to bed," Mom explained. She squeezed my hand. "He didn't mean to yell at you, sweetie."

"You don't have to apologize for him," I said. "He should apologize for himself."

She sighed and pinched the spot between her eyes. "Ready to open your presents?"

I said I was. And I decided that actually it was better opening them without my disgusting little brother and my father who hated me and would never apologize to me in this lifetime. There was a box of stationery from Andy. Mom and Dad had given me a nice red sweater with snowflakes on it. And a camera. I already knew I wasn't getting what I really wanted — a computer — so I tried not to be disappointed, even though I really was.

Sam gave me a beautiful journal with a tapestry cover — to write all my stories and ideas in, he said. That was a really great present.

I saved David's present for last. Just as I was about to tear the ribbons off the huge box, the doorbell rang. David ran to get it. I got a bad feeling in the pit of my stomach.

"Foreboding," Sam said. "Noun. Uninvited dread."

David came back into the dining room with his arm around *her*. She carried a gift-wrapped present.

"Look who's here!" David said, just too cheerful.

"It's Uninvited Dread!" Sam chirped.

"What a nice surprise." Mom smiled at Jayne.

"Thanks," the J-word replied. David helped her off with her jacket. "It got cold out, huh?"

Across the table, Sam did his Frankenstein imitation.

The J-word turned to me. "I hope you don't mind that Davie invited me to crash your party, Darce."

"Don't call me Darce," I said icily. "*Davie* is the only one who calls me that."

"Oh. Sorry." She held the gift out to me. "Happy birthday."

What could I do? I had to take it. I tore off the paper. Inside was a book. *The Member of the Wedding*, by Carson McCullers.

"It's number twenty-eight on your list, isn't it?" the J-word asked eagerly. "That's what Davie told me."

How could he have told her about Meemaw's book list? It was *private*. But probably nothing was private anymore. David thought he could just share all our secrets with her.

"It's very nice," I forced myself to say. "Thanks."

"Now open mine," David said eagerly. He pulled out a chair for the J-word, and the two of them sat down.

I tore the paper off the big box and opened it. Inside was a huge stuffed bear with a goofy face.

"Look at his neck, Darce," David urged me.

I did. Around the bear's neck was a heart-shaped necklace on a slender gold chain. David got up and lifted the chain off the bear. Then he put it around my neck.

"Oh, Dee Dee, that's so pretty," my mom said.

I lifted the heart to look at it. It really *was* pretty.

"Like it?" David asked.

"Yeah," I admitted. It was such a great present, I couldn't help smiling. "I'm going to wear it all the time."

"Why don't you go show Dad?" Mom asked me.

She sounded so hopeful, and David's present was just so terrific, that I decided I would be big enough to forgive my father.

"Okay." I took off toward my parents' room.

"Wait, Dee Dee," Jayne called to me. "Look at this!" She reached under the neckline of her sweater and lifted something out. It was a slender gold chain, and on the end of it was a heart, exactly like mine. "Davie got me the same necklace. Isn't that so great? It's almost like we're sisters!"

"I don't want a sister," I spat at her. "And if I did, it wouldn't be you."

"Oops," Sam squeaked.

"Darcy, what a horrible thing to say," my mother exclaimed. "You apologize!"

"No." I folded my arms. "You can't make me."

"You are impossible," my mother declared, throwing her hands in the air.

"Good," I said. "I want to be impossible."

Mom turned to the J-word. "I apologize for her, Jayne."

"Oh, it's okay," the J-word said softly. "I understand."

David gave her this disgusting look of love, then he squeezed her hand.

I felt like smacking her.

I pushed my chair back. "Well, I kind of have this headache now so I'm going to bed. Thanks, everyone, for the nice birthday."

"Dee Dee, you're being very rude —" my mom began.

"Darce, wait," David said. "Jayne and I are going over to the park. There's a jazz concert — last one of the season — we thought you and Sam could —"

"Like I said, I have this bad headache."

My mother shrugged helplessly to David and Jayne, but I ignored her. I gathered up my gifts, went to my room, got undressed, turned off the light, and crawled into bed. A phrase I had read in some book popped into my head: tattered pride.

That's what I had. Tattered pride.

And it was all *her* fault.

I must have fallen asleep, because I woke up with a start, my mind all foggy. Something bad had happened, hadn't it?

And then I remembered.

David had brought *her* to my birthday party, without even asking me. He had given *her* the same necklace he'd given me. He loved her.

And I wasn't ever going to be able to break them up.

My luminous alarm clock read nine-thirty. That meant David and the J-word were probably still at the park. Two halves that made up a complete whole, with no room for me.

I fingered the heart around my neck. I was twelve now. Not a little kid. Even if I looked about eight on the outside, it was time to grow up on the inside.

I would go to the park and apologize to them. I'd wish them every happiness.

And I'd try hard to mean it.

In the dark, I tugged on my jeans, put on my new snowflake sweater for luck, pushed into my sneakers, and wound a scrunchie around my hair.

The house was dark and silent. So far so good. There was a chance I could sneak out without my parents hearing me. I opened the front door the tiniest bit.

Quickly, carefully, I tiptoed into the night.

The cold hit me like an unexpected slap. I stuck my hands inside the sleeves of my new sweater as I hurried the ten blocks to the park. The jazz music from the outdoor bandshell grew louder.

I walked quickly through the crowd, scanning faces, looking for David and the J-word. The crowd around the bandshell wasn't very big — most people had already left. The band would stop playing soon.

I didn't see them. So I wandered to the other side of the park, where a huge stone fountain, surrounded by benches, was illuminated by old-fashioned streetlights. Some friends of David's called to me, and I waved at them, but no David.

Just when I thought they weren't in the park at all, I saw form and movement, on a bench far from the others. Somehow I knew it was them. I was right. They were wrapped in each other's arms.

They were kissing.

I melted into the shadows behind them.

After a while, she pulled away from him, lifting her heart-shaped necklace to admire it. "I love this so much."

David put his forehead against hers. "I guess this means you've got my heart."

"I'm so glad I talked you into getting Darcy a matching necklace," she said.

"I don't know why," David said. "She acted like a real brat."

"This is hard on her, Davie. She's just a kid, and she worships you. She wants to be with you all the time."

"Believe me, I know," David groaned. He put his arms around her again. "So let's take advantage of the fact that she's not here now."

The J-word laughed. They started kissing again.

I stepped out of the shadows.

She saw me first.

"Darce!" She pushed some mussed hair off her face.

"I told you not to call me that," I said coldly.

David just looked at me, his arms around *her*. "What are you doing here?"

"Watching."

He made a noise of exasperation in the back of his throat. "Look, we invited you to come and you didn't want to. So now, this is kind of . . . private."

"Oh, I can see that," I said nastily. "It's amazing

63

what you find out listening in on a *private* conversation."

"Darce —" David began.

"I came here to *apologize*," I shouted. "And what did I find out? The necklace you gave me wasn't even your idea. It was *her* idea."

"What difference does it make whose idea it was?"

"I didn't invite her to my birthday!" I yelled at him. "Who gave you the right to invite her?"

"Hey, Darce, it isn't like you to be mean like this," David said, holding his beloved even closer.

"I *am* mean. I've always been mean."

Inside I felt hot and ugly, full of some terrible poison that had to come out, I couldn't stop it, I didn't *want* to stop it.

"I hate her," I said.

"You don't mean that, Darce —"

"I d-do mean it," I stuttered, my mind a sea of red. "I hate her guts. And I hate your guts, too. I w-wish you were dead!"

I tore off the heart-shaped necklace and threw it at him with all my might. Then I turned and ran toward the street.

Tears blinded me, but I kept running, hard and fast. From a ways behind me, I heard David calling to me.

"Darce!" he yelled. "Darce!"

I could hear his footsteps, growing closer, gaining on me. I ran even faster, as fast as I could. I got

64

to the street and darted out between two parked cars. I wouldn't let him catch me, no, never. I would run out of my own skin, until I became someone else, anyone else but awful me.

"Darce!" David called again. "Stop so I can —"

That's when I heard the terrible noise from behind me: brakes squealing, a sickening thud, and then a silence far more terrifying than the sounds that had come before.

I stood on the other side of the street, panting so hard I thought my lungs would rip out of my throat.

If I didn't turn around, it wouldn't be true.

A car door slammed.

"Oh, my God, he darted right out in front of me!" a horrified voice yelled.

"Is he dead?"

"I've got a cell phone, I'll call 911!"

Did I run back? I must have but I don't remember. All I know is that I was there, next to him. And all I remember is the streetlight, shining down on the crumpled, mangled, bloody body of my brother.

7

Two months later

"**H**ave a seat," Annie Preston said, waving me toward the couch in her office. "You can call me Annie, by the way."

She was short and round with a pretty face and red hair the color of autumn leaves before they die. I could picture her hair turning brown and crisp, then crackling and falling off of her head.

Everything dies, you know.

I sat on the very edge of the chair, clutching my journal, the one Sam had given me on my birthday.

Annie sat across from me. "Well, Darcy, is there anything you'd like to say?"

"You d-don't look old enough to be a psychologist."

She laughed. "Yeah, everyone tells me that. But I'm thirty. And you're —?"

"Twelve."

She nodded and waited. So did I. I knew I could out-wait her.

"Your mom told me on the phone that you stopped eating a couple of days ago," she finally said. "You must be hungry."

I shrugged.

"Really? I'd be hungry if I didn't eat for two days."

I shrugged again.

"What's that you're holding?"

"My journal."

"May I see it?"

I had brought it with me so I wouldn't have to talk about what had happened. I handed it to her.

She opened it. A newspaper article with David's picture was glued to the first page.

STAR HS ATHLETE DEETON HIT
BY CAR, CRITICALLY INJURED

(Appleton, Sept. 17) Appleton West High School's star halfback, David Deeton, 18, is in a coma and listed in critical condition at Green Bay Memorial Hospital. He was critically injured when a car hit him in an automobile-pedestrian accident on College Street, near Houdini Park, yesterday evening. Deeton was life-flighted to GBMH's new trauma unit. There will be a hospital news conference on Deeton's condition at 6:00 P.M. tomorrow.

Deeton apparently darted out into the

street between parked cars before he was hit. A preliminary investigation has led police to conclude this was an accident, and no charges have been filed against the driver of the vehicle.

Almost immediately after the accident, as word spread through the community, friends and classmates of the popular young athlete came together at the fountain in Houdini Park, creating a silent, candlelight vigil in honor of their fallen classmate.

Annie looked up at me, then she turned the page and read the next article I'd glued into my journal.

LIFE-SUPPORT REMOVED, DEETON PRONOUNCED DEAD
Athlete's Organs Rushed for Transplants

(Green Bay, Sept. 25) The weeklong ordeal of Appleton West High School's star halfback David Deeton, 18, ended tragically yesterday, as Deeton's parents and doctors at Green Bay Memorial Hospital agreed to turn off the respirator which had been keeping him alive.

Deeton had signed an organ donation card and his parents complied with his wishes. Doctors prepared Deeton's heart, corneas, and kidneys for transplant, and all have been flown to various hospitals around the country.

Deeton was critically injured when a car hit him near Houdini Park on September 16.

The popular high school senior, who received severe trauma to his head in the accident, never regained consciousness nor showed brain wave activity.

The scores of people touched by Deeton's plight, who have held an around-the-clock prayer vigil in Houdini Park since the accident, were devastated when told the news. "Dave Deeton was perhaps the finest young man it has ever been my pleasure to know," Appleton West High School football coach Brad Majors said, when told of Deeton's death. "This is a tremendous loss to us all."

A public memorial service is planned for tomorrow, at 10:00 A.M. at Appleton West High School football field. Brett Favre, Green Bay Packers quarterback, will speak, as will Mayor Leeson and community religious leaders. Private burial services will follow the memorial. In lieu of flowers, donations may be made to the David Deeton Fund, created by the family and friends of the deceased, to support local athletics.

Annie sighed and shook her head, then she turned to the next page. There, I had glued a print of the last photo ever taken of David, with his arm around me at my birthday dinner.

My birthday. His deathday.

After that, the journal was blank.

Like me.

"I'm so sorry about your brother's death." She handed me my journal. "Were you there when it happened?"

My heartbeat sped up. I didn't say anything.

"You were there, weren't you?" she probed.

"No."

"Maybe I got it wrong, then. Your mom told me —"

"I w-wasn't. I left before."

"Before the accident?"

I clutched my journal harder. "I d-didn't s-see anything."

She nodded, waiting for me to explain.

"I d-don't want to talk about it," I said quickly.

"You might feel better if you did." She waited again.

I didn't speak.

"Your mom told me you haven't cried."

I shrugged.

She made a tent with her fingers. "On the night of the accident, when you went to the park —"

I jumped out of the chair. "I *s-said* I d-don't want to *t-talk* about it! Can't you *hear*? Are you *deaf*?"

For a moment, she just looked at me. "All right. You don't have to talk about it if you don't want to."

I looked right back at her. I didn't sit down. If she brought up that night again, I would just leave. She couldn't force me to stay.

Annie leaned toward me. "You don't have to do or say anything in here unless you choose to, Darcy. You're the one in control. And nothing you tell me will be repeated to anyone, unless you want me to."

I nodded guardedly.

"Sometimes, when a tragic accident occurs," she went on, "it helps to talk about it. So whenever you decide you're ready to talk, I want you to know that I'll be ready to listen."

She was going to be waiting a really long time. I was *never* going to talk about it.

She would never understand: how I lay in bed every night, staring out my window at the stars, trying not to think how it was hard to breathe because of this weight on my chest. I couldn't sleep. Because if I slept, the weight on my chest might crush me, just because it was what I deserved.

But not if I stayed awake, vigilant, and kept breathing; in, out, in, out.

I wasn't about to tell Annie Preston any of that.

I wasn't about to tell anyone.

I'd rather *die* than tell what had really happened that night.

The police had interviewed a lot of the people who'd been in the park, but no one had seen what had happened. The only person besides me who knew the truth was Jayne. And even though my parents and the police and all Jayne's friends had asked her over and over what had happened, why David had run out onto College Street between parked cars without looking, she never told.

But she never spoke to me, either. Not at the funeral. Not when she came over to visit my parents.

Everyone called it a tragic accident, but Jayne and I knew better.

It was murder.

And I was the murderer.

8

The next day was Thanksgiving.

It's a stupid holiday when you have nothing to be thankful for.

My mom made a turkey, and we sat silently around the dining room table, chewing.

I took a bite of stuffing and hated myself for doing it. Although I knew I deserved to suffer and die for what I had done, and starvation seemed like a good way to do it, I was too weak-willed. I had started eating again.

Our house was filled with the weight of suffocating silence. The air itself felt heavy. Breathing took effort; talk was almost impossible.

I hated being home, and rode my bike for hours or hid out at the library. My father's hair had turned gray. His back was worse. My mom stopped working out and started smoking cigarettes. She drank too much wine at dinner. When she laughed, it was always at things that weren't funny. Andy got into fights at school. He got in-school suspension three times.

Before, Dad would have grounded him for that forever.

Now, Dad did nothing. Because nothing mattered.

I chewed some dry turkey. The turkey had once been alive. Then someone killed it, so that we could eat it.

I spit it into my napkin. No one said a word.

The room was so quiet. David's chair was still pulled up to the table. His photo still hung on the wall. His sports trophies were on the mantle.

He was everywhere, but nowhere.

Dad pushed his chair back. "I have some work to do at the station house."

"But we all go see Meemaw on Thanksgiving and Christmas," I reminded him.

I didn't say this because I wanted to go. I said it because I felt so guilty that I didn't.

Ever since the accident, the same mean thought about Meemaw ran through my mind over and over: Why aren't you dead instead of David?

"I'll be late," Dad told Mom. "No need to wait up." Then he left.

Mom sighed as she got up. "Well, that's that, then. Kids, help me clean up, please."

"I'm gonna go watch the Lions game," Andy said, running out of the room.

Mom didn't say a word. She just carried some dirty plates into the kitchen.

In silence, I helped her clean up. When only the turkey pan was left to scrub, I said I'd do it, so Mom went into her room and shut the door.

I washed the pan. I knew what I should do next — put on my coat, get on my bike, and go see Meemaw.

It's what David would have wanted me to do.

I put on my coat and walked out the door. It was late afternoon, the sky was gloomy, the temperature below freezing. A light dusting of snow had fallen the night before. But the streets were clear, so I pulled on my mittens, got on my bike, and headed down our driveway. But then, as if my bike had a mind of its own, it turned into Sam's driveway.

Sam and I hadn't spent much time together. He and his parents had come to the funeral. For the week after that, Sam's parents let him skip school, and he came over and hung out with me every day. I didn't want to talk, so we didn't. A lot of the time, we just sat there. But I felt better, having him around.

Then I started thinking, what right did I have to feel better when David couldn't feel anything at all? So I yelled at Sam to leave. And not to come back. Ever.

Since then, I had only seen him at school. He

took the bus home every day with those two mental giants, Henry Farmer and Amanda Bliss.

I knocked on the Weiss's front door. Sam's dad opened it. From the dining room I could hear a lot of people talking and laughing.

"Dee Dee!" Mr. Weiss exclaimed. "Come on in." He held the glass door open for me. "How're you doing?"

People always asked me that. But I knew that none of them really wanted to know the truth.

"Okay." I took off my mittens. "Is Sam here?"

There was a loud burst of laughter from the dining room, the sound of people who have never been lonely.

"I guess you're eating now," I said. "I should go —"

"No, no, don't leave," Mr. Weiss said quickly. "I'll get Sam. Or you could come in and join us."

I just stared at him.

"I'm very sorry about your brother."

"That was two months ago," I said coldly.

"I know," he said gently. "I was at the funeral. I just wanted you to know how sorry I am that —"

"Why should you be sorry? Your son is fine. Your life is just terrific."

"Dee Dee." His voice was gentle. He put his arm around my shoulder. Bette came into the hallway and looked at me with concern.

There was another burst of laughter from the

dining room, from all the people who belonged, who weren't murderers.

I pulled away from Mr. Weiss. "I have to go."

"Don't go, Dee Dee," Bette said. "I understand. I'll get Sam —"

But I was already out the door.

I was back on my bike and halfway down the long driveway, when Sam called to me.

"Hey, Deed!"

I kept going.

"I don't have a jacket on, ya know!" he yelled. "If I catch pneumonia, it'll be your fault."

I circled around and biked back to him. He stood there, looking so puny and skinny and dumb, so Sam-like, that I wanted to cry.

"Only a dork would come outside without a jacket when it's this cold, Sam," I told him.

"I was highly motivated," he said, shivering.

His mother stuck her head out the door holding Sam's jacket. "It's freezing out. Put your jacket on! Or would you two rather come in and have dessert with us?"

"Go for door number one," I told him.

He went to get his jacket and hurried back over to me, climbing on my handlebars. "So, let's go," he said.

"Go where? It's Thanksgiving. Everything is closed."

"You see, Deed, this shows you continue to lack imagination," Sam said. "Head for the Metamorphosis statue. It's time we communed with Houdini."

"What for?"

Sam looked at me like the answer was obvious. "For David, of course."

I don't know why I let him talk me into it. Maybe because I didn't really want to go to see Meemaw, and I didn't want to go home, either. Home was full of ghosts. Any place was better than that.

By the time we got to Houdini Plaza, it was dark, and I was so cold I couldn't feel my face.

"This was a dumb idea," I said, jumping up and down to try and warm up.

"In a moment, you won't feel the cold," Sam assured me. "Okay, we have to sit under the statue. Then we have to close our eyes and clear our minds of everything." He sat and closed his eyes.

"What for?"

He opened his eyes. "Because Houdini's spirit can't get in if your mind is already filled."

I put my freezing hands in my armpits. "Sam, Houdini is dead."

"I heard. Now, what you need to do is —"

"You told me yourself that after Houdini's mother died, he tried to reach her over and over, but he couldn't. When you're dead, you're just . . . dead."

Sam folded his arms. "So you're telling me that

you don't want Houdini's help in talking to David?"

My throat ached from the cold. "No one can do that," I said, gulping hard. "Not even Houdini."

"What if you're wrong?"

"I'm not."

"But what if you are?"

Suddenly I filled up with a terrible rage. "Don't you get it? I'm never, ever, *ever* going to get to talk to David again. So just admit it."

"But —"

"Just admit it, Sam. Admit it or you can't ride home on my bike!"

"I can't admit something I don't —"

"Fine, then. Walk home. You can freeze to death, for all I care."

"Deed —"

I ran as fast as I could toward my bike, which I'd left leaning against a tree, but I hit an ice patch and went down hard, my ankle twisting under me.

"Are you okay?" Sam went to help me up.

"No." I pushed him away and struggled up on my own, keeping weight off my right ankle. "Why did I come here with you, anyway? What a stupid idea."

I took a step. My right ankle gave way. I fell again. My anger was a life raft. I wouldn't let go. "Look what you did, Sam."

He knelt down to me. "I'll call my parents. It's okay, Deed —"

"It *isn't* okay! *Nothing* is okay. I'll never get to talk to David again, no matter what. My life will just go on and on and on, because I'm too chicken to stop breathing, and I'll never get to tell him —"

"Tell him what?"

That I'm sorry I killed him, I thought. *That I'd give anything in the world to take back the words I said to him that night. Or to hear him say he could forgive me.*

But I couldn't say any of that aloud. Not ever.

I wrapped my arms around myself. "I want to die," I whispered. "I wish I were dead."

Sam didn't say anything. He just wrapped his skinny arms around me, a very un-Sam-like thing to do.

For a while we just sat there on the freezing-cold ground. Finally, Sam got up and pulled me up, too.

I couldn't look at him. "This does not count as our first date, okay?"

He couldn't look at me, either. "K-O." He cleared his throat just like his father does. "I can confirm that your heart is still beating, so it appears your petition to die has been denied. Now, here's what we should do . . ."

Sam kept talking, but I wasn't listening. Because the strangest thing had happened.

Suddenly, I wasn't cold anymore.

My ankle didn't even hurt.

"Uh, Deed? Did you hear me? I said I'm walking over to that pay phone and —"

"My heart is still beating," I said, full of wonder.

"Agreed. So first I'll help you over to the statue. You can sit there while I go call my parents. Then —"

"Sam, shut up a minute. Don't you get it? *Some-one else's heart is still beating, too.*"

His eyes met mine. A light dawned.

"A person whose heart is still beating isn't really dead," I went on. "You just said so your-self."

Sam nodded.

"Somewhere, David's heart is still beating. Which means that in a way, he's still alive."

I grabbed Sam's hands in mine. There was a new feeling inside of me, as if I'd been trapped in the darkest, scariest place, and someone had fi-nally turned on a light.

"We can do it. I know we can." I squished Sam's fingers between mine. "We have to find David's heart. Please say you'll help me. Sam?"

I waited.

Then he got a very Sam-like smile on his face. And all he said was: "K-O."

9

Once when I was little, I found this baby bird in our backyard. It was so tiny and fragile. David helped me make a nest for it in a shoe box. I took really good care of that bird. I watched over it and fed it with an eyedropper every few hours. But I guess it was too little and weak, because one morning I woke up and looked into the shoe box and the bird had died. David and I held a funeral and buried it in the backyard.

It seems to me that hope is like that bird. For a while, I took really good care of my new, hopeful feeling. During the next few weeks, Sam and I spent all our free time trying to find out who had my brother's heart. But with every blind alley, and every dead end, my hope got smaller and weaker. If something good didn't happen soon, I knew it was only a matter of time before I'd be holding a funeral for it in the backyard.

On the outside, I acted normal. Mom asked me how things were going with Annie Preston, who I saw twice a week after school. I said fine. During the day I did all the things I usually did. Went to school. Did my chores. Hung out with Sam. Did my homework.

But at night, I lay there, staring out my window at the stars, listening to myself breathe; in, out, in, out. And I would think: If I stop doing this, I will die.

Not sleeping makes you tired, and being tired makes you let down your guard, which is why it was getting harder and harder to not tell Annie anything important. Like how I worried that I'd stop breathing. Or that I didn't sleep anymore.

Or that I was a murderer.

I didn't tell her about looking for David's heart. The only person who knew was Sam, and I had sworn him to secrecy.

One day at school I was so tired I fell asleep while Mrs. Pritcher was at the blackboard diagramming sentences. After class, she took me aside. "Time heals everything, Dee Dee," she told me. Then she gave me a hug.

What a stupid thing to say. Time does *not* heal everything. There are some things that nothing can heal.

We were in Sam's bedroom, and he was sitting in the trunk we used for the Metamorphosis trick. We had brought all the magic stuff back over to his house, since I didn't want to spend any more time at my house than I had to. Not that I cared about working on escape tricks. But Sam did.

I sat at Sam's computer, typing in some words. There was only one day of school left before winter vacation, and we were no closer to finding David's heart than we had been three weeks ago.

"I'm using a search engine again, to look for heart transplants," I told him, as I typed it into his computer.

He had locked his wrists in handcuffs, and was trying to open them with a picklock he held between his teeth.

"Did you hear me?" I asked him.

"M-hm." His teeth were clenched so as not to drop the picklock, which he was carefully maneuvering into the keyhole of the handcuffs.

"I'll try 'waiting list,' too." I typed it in.

"Got it!" Sam yelled triumphantly, as the handcuffs sprang open. "That was my best time yet."

"Are you going to come help me or not?"

Sam stepped out of the trunk. "Your turn."

"I'm not getting in the trunk."

Something was coming up on the computer screen at a website to which the search engine had directed me. "Transplant information is confidential," the screen read.

That's what the screen *always* read.

Sam climbed on top of the trunk so he could see himself better in the mirror over his dresser, and he put on one of the half-dozen pairs of sunglasses

Bette had just given him for Hanukkah. Sam collects sunglasses. Who knows why. It's a Sam thing.

"The name is Bond. James Bond," he told his reflection.

"The name is Moron. Big Moron." I rubbed my eyes. I was so tired. I couldn't remember anymore what it felt like not to be tired.

I stared at his computer. There had to be a way to find David's heart. There just had to be.

We had already surfed through a zillion websites and newsgroups about heart transplants. We had found the history of transplants, medical descriptions of transplants, foundations that supported transplants, even an organization that said organ transplants were against God's will.

We had tried everything on the Internet and off. We called Green Bay Memorial Hospital, but the woman in charge of organ transplants told us transplant information was confidential. The recipient could decide to contact the donor's family, but it was the recipient's choice. Sam had even tried to hack his way into the hospital's organ donor computer files, but that kind of thing works much better in the movies than it does in real life.

"Maybe there's some key word that we just haven't thought of," I mused.

"I doubt it." Sam switched to another pair of sunglasses. These were zebra-striped. "Do these make me look taller?"

"Look, are you going to help me or —"

"Hey, I thought you told me you were going to study your Hebrew," Mr. Weiss said, sticking his head in the door.

"The Great Samdini is taking a well-deserved break," Sam boomed, staring at his father through the zebra-striped sunglasses.

Mr. Weiss looked skeptical. "Well, the father of the Great Samdini expects your Hebrew book to magically appear, and those sunglasses to magically *dis*appear. You're on your honor, Sam. Your mom and I have to go to a meeting in Green Bay and we won't be home until nine or ten. Bette is downstairs. She's going to have dinner with you. Okay?"

"K-O," Sam agreed.

"Tomorrow you and I are working on your Hebrew together," Mr. Weiss added before he left.

"By the time I'm eighteen I'll be speaking Hebrew, French, and ancient Greek fluently," Sam said, pawing through his sunglass collection. "All self-taught off the computer, of course." He put on a gold pair with wings and admired his reflection. "These give me something of a Greek-god look, don't you think? Keep in mind that all Greek gods were short, and that I have a very fragile ego."

"You're a disturbed person," I told him. "Help me look for new websites."

"Kids, you hungry?" Bette asked from the doorway. She's a jewelry designer, and as usual she had on a few of her large, original pieces. At the moment she was munching on a homemade cookie and carrying a ceramic mug of coffee.

"If it's got sugar in it, the Great Samdini is always hungry," I told her.

She laughed. "Well, then the Great Samdini is in luck. I baked for my yoga class but they broke out in hives when I admitted to using white flour. Your mom made lentil stew, Sam, which speaks for itself. I suggest we dine on cookies and banana bread. Can you join us, Dee Dee?"

"I have to go home for dinner, but thanks."

"I'll give you some to take home." She popped the last bite of cookie into her mouth, and peered at me. "You look so tired, sweetie."

"I'm okay."

She came over to me and put her cool hand on my cheek. "Of course you're not okay," she said tenderly. Her hand was so soft on my cheek. If she just kept it there, I could close my eyes, and not think about my breathing, and sleep.

She took her hand away.

"So, how's the Hebrew going?" she asked Sam, sipping her coffee.

He moseyed over to the computer. "Auspiciously. Adverb. Showing signs of success."

"Glad to hear it." She glanced idly at the computer screen. Sam quickly blacked out the website list.

"Computers are amazing, aren't they?" she

marveled. "Did you happen to read the article in this morning's newspaper about the new Compaq notebooks?"

"No, Bette," Sam said. "I was too busy sleeping through what is laughingly referred to as school."

Bette raised an eyebrow. "This may come as a shock to you, but there really are adults who can teach you something."

"Perhaps," Sam agreed. "But sadly none of them teach at my school."

"All the more reason, Boy Genius, for you to be reading the newspaper every day." She sipped her coffee and smacked her lips. "I'm sorry, but no decaf in the world compares with the real thing. Let me know when you're hungry, Sam." She left.

I looked at my watch. "My mom's doing another double shift, so I have to go home and start dinner in exactly ten minutes. Now, are you going to help me or not?" I touched a key and the website list reappeared on the screen.

Suddenly, Sam hit himself in the forehead. "I'm an idiot."

"Agreed. I'm down to nine minutes and thirty-nine seconds, Sam."

"Bette was just talking about the *newspaper*. *Newspaper* search, Deed! It's so simple! Nexus!"

I stared at him blankly.

"Nexus is an on-line system that uses key words to search the text of just about any newspaper in the country. I used it at computer camp!"

"Uh-huh," I said, not following him at all. "And?"

"Think about it. We know what day David's heart got harvested, early morning of September 25th, right?"

Something turned in my stomach. "Harvested" was the right term — I knew that from all the research we'd done — but it sounded so awful.

"We know his heart was flown to wherever the transplant was going to be done," Sam went on, "and we know that the recipient would have been prepped and in surgery when the heart arrived, right?"

"Right," I agreed.

"So that means someone got David's heart on September 25th," Sam rushed on. "If we key in that date and some other key words, and do a universal search on all the newspapers in the country, doesn't it make sense that an article might have appeared about this person getting a new heart?"

Maybe. It was at least *possible*.

I put my hands over my heart, where hope was busy proving it wasn't dead yet at all. "So, do you have this Nexus thing on your computer?"

"No," Sam admitted, but he had the biggest grin on his face. "But I just happen to know someone who does."

10

"This is never going to work," I said nervously, as Sam and I walked into the lobby of the building downtown where his parents worked. He was carrying a huge, gift-wrapped box.

"It'll work," Sam insisted. "What time is it?"

I looked at my watch. "Eight o'clock."

"Perfect. I know my parents said Mr. Epps switched to the night shift. He should have just come on duty."

We rounded the corner. Ahead of us, near the elevators, was a simple wooden desk, behind which sat a large black security guard.

"That's Mr. Epps?" I hissed.

Sam nodded.

"You didn't tell me he was black."

Sam looked at me like I was crazy. "And that would be relevant because . . . ?"

"Nothing," I mumbled. Sam was right. It didn't matter. And before my father started blaming

Charles Jordan's race for everything, I never would have even thought about it.

"Hey, Mr. Epps, how's it going?" Sam asked, as we approached the desk. "Remember me? Ed and Sarah Weiss's kid? We met last year when you were on the day shift, when my parents brought me on Take Your Kid to Work Day? I got bored up in their office, and I came down and played chess with you?"

Mr. Epps rubbed his chin for a moment, then he snapped his fingers. "Sure, I remember you! Sam, isn't it?"

"Great memory! Oh, this is my friend... Amanda Bliss," he added brightly.

Amanda Bliss?

I gave Mr. Epps a sickly smile. He nodded at me.

"So, Mr. Epps, how's the missus?" Sam asked.

"I'm divorced, Sam."

"Oh yeah? Me, too!" Sam laughed too heartily at his lame joke. He leaned toward Mr. Epps. "So listen, I have this huge favor to ask you. See, this is a Jewish holiday called Hanukkah. We light candles for eight nights in honor of this miracle, where —"

"Sam, my daughter married a Jewish fellow," Mr. Epps interrupted. "I'm up to speed on the miracle. So what can I do for you?"

Sam tapped his finger against the huge, gift-wrapped box, which he had set on the desktop. "Well, see, I got this big model of the scales of justice for my parents. It's a special one they've always wanted. But it kind of has to be assembled. And I really want to surprise them. So I was wondering if I could go up to their office and, you know, assemble it."

"No way, no how," Mr. Epps said firmly. "Sorry, young man. I could get fired for that."

"But if you could just make an exception this once," Sam pleaded. "It would mean so much to my parents, and —"

"Hey, Sam!"

We turned around. A middle-aged man in a tweed coat, carrying a briefcase, was walking toward us.

"Hi, Mr. Laugen," Sam said.

"What are you doing here? I thought your parents went to the bar association meeting in Green Bay."

"They did," Sam said. "This is my friend, Dee . . . Aman-*dee* Bliss. This is Larry Laugen; he works with my parents."

"Hi," I said.

"Were you just on your way up to the office?" Sam asked hopefully.

Mr. Laugen nodded, and tapped his briefcase. "Death penalty appeal. I'm burning the midnight oil on this one. Why, what's up?"

Sam repeated his story about assembling the model as a surprise Hanukkah gift for his parents.

"No prob," Mr. Laugen said. "Come on up with me."

"As long as he's your responsibility, Mr. Laugen," Mr. Epps said.

"Hey, I've known this kid forever, it's okay." Mr. Laugen ruffled Sam's hair.

Sam really hates that. But he just smiled.

We rode up in the elevator, then Mr. Laugen unlocked the double doors to the offices. "You want your mom's office or your dad's?"

"Mom's is fine," Sam said. "I know where it is."

"Just holler at me before you leave, okay?"

"Sure thing," Sam agreed.

We hurried to Sam's mom's office and closed the door. Sam threw the gift-wrapped box, which was empty, on the couch, then he booted up his mom's computer.

"Can we g-get arrested for this?" I asked him.

"If we get busted, I'm reasonably sure my mother will defend us." He deftly punched keys on the keyboard.

"That's comforting." I paced nervously while Sam got into Nexus. I'd told my father that I had a stomachache, and went to bed right after dinner. Mom was at the hospital, Andy was in his room and my father was in my parents' bedroom with the TV on when I had snuck out of the house.

If my father found out, he'd kill me.

"Bingo, piece of cake!" Sam said. "We're in."

I rushed to him and looked over his shoulder.

He typed in the date, September 25, and the year. Then he told the computer to search for "heart" in the same article as "transplant" and "high school athlete" and "Wisconsin."

"Now let's hope we get lucky," Sam muttered. He punched a single key, hard.

We waited. And waited. And waited.

"Come on, come on, come on," I chanted, willing the computer to go faster.

"Hey, how's it going in there?" Mr. Laugen called from the hallway.

Sam and I traded panicked looks.

I ran to the door and quickly locked it from the inside. "Fine!" I called to him.

"When do I get to see the big surprise?" Mr. Laugen asked. "I wish my kids were as thoughtful as you are, Sam."

"He's . . . p-putting it together now," I called through the door. "He's . . . concentrating."

"Okay. Yell if you need anything."

"Okay!" I called. "Thanks!" I ran back over to Sam. "He wants to see the model. What are we going to do?"

"Got me." Sam's eyes were glued to the screen.

And then, finally, a short list appeared on the screen. Three articles from three different newspapers, all containing the key words.

My heart fell. The first two were from newspapers in Appleton and Green Bay. And they were about David.

Which left us only one chance in the entire world.

"Do it," I told Sam, crossing my fingers for luck.

He pressed a key. A small article from the Miami *Herald* appeared on the screen.

WINSTON PAWLING, AGE 12, GETS NEW HEART

Miami Beach youth Winston Pawling, a 12-year-old home-schooled student who formerly attended Holy Trinity School, received a heart transplant yesterday at the University of Pittsburgh Medical Center.

Pawling, who had a congenital heart condition, had been waiting in Pittsburgh with his parents for three months in hopes that an organ would become available. A star high school athlete in Wisconsin, 18, who had been fatally injured when he was hit by a car, was the donor.

Pawling is the son of Miami physicians John Paul and Linda Pawling. Both took a leave of absence to be with their son in Pittsburgh while he awaited a donor match. Winston was reported in good condition after his surgery. He and his parents will return to Miami when Winston is released from the hospital.

My whole body was trembling. I just kept staring at the screen.

Winston Pawling. Some kid named Winston Pawling had my brother's heart. Right that very minute.

"That's pay dirt, Deed," Sam said, his voice hushed.

"I never thought it would be a kid."

"Me, neither."

In a daze, I went over to the couch and sat down. "Write down all the information, okay?"

"K-O." Sam grabbed a pen.

"What we have to do next is obvious," I told him. "You know that, right?"

Sam hesitated for a moment. "Miami, huh?" he finally said. "What luck. I can make use of my new sunglasses."

"I only have twenty-four dollars in my piggy bank," I realized. "That won't get us very far."

"It so happens that I'm flush at the moment. Hanukkah *gelt* that hasn't gone into the bank yet. Bette gives cash. It's a family tradition. When do we leave?"

"Tomorrow morning," I decided, thinking hard. "Take the bus to school, I'll take my bike. Then we'll take my bike to the depot downtown and ditch it someplace. That way our parents won't know we're gone until later. We'll have a good head start. Pack as much food as you can in your backpack, and I will, too."

We just sat there, not speaking, both of us thinking about what we were about to do.

"I'll pay you back, Sam. One day. I promise."

"The Great Samdini is not too hung up on money," he boomed in his Great-Samdini voice. "Consider it a gift."

"Some gifts are worth more than all the money in the world, Sam. Thank you."

He nodded. "You're welcome."

Sam was shivering from the cold night air when he got off the handlebars of my bike. A warm, amber light bathed the front porch. The electric Hanukkah menorah in the front window radiated a steady orange glow.

His eyes met mine. We didn't speak. I turned my bike around and he walked into his house.

My house was completely dark. I wheeled my bike into the open garage, and went around to the front door, because the door that leads in from the garage squeaks.

As I tiptoed in, I held my breath. Everything was black and silent.

I was halfway through the living room when I heard my father's voice.

"It's almost Christmas," he said eerily.

His voice had come from the couch.

I froze. I was in so much trouble.

"We don't have a tree. Last year we had that big tree," Dad went on. "Remember? We put this gold football at the top — D. DEETON #17, it says on it — I forget who made it for us."

He sounded so strange. It was him, but not him. As my eyes adjusted to the dark, I could make out his silhouette on the couch. The big cardboard box we kept in the basement, which held our Christmas ornaments, was open at his feet. He was holding the gold satin football, stitched with D. DEETON #17, in his big hands.

"I'm s-sorry I went over to Sam's without p-permission," I said.

He didn't seem to hear me.

"Remember this?" He held up something else from the box — a ceramic angel that, before last year, used to go at the top of the tree. "My mother gave it to your mom and me on our wedding day. I always hated it."

I couldn't move. Like a dead butterfly in someone's collection, I was pinned to the spot by my father's eerie voice.

"I'm sorry I couldn't get you a computer for Christmas this year. If I had gotten that promotion . . ."

"It's okay."

"I know that's what you want. My mother never got me what I wanted for Christmas. She got me books instead. I vowed I wouldn't be like that with my own kids."

"That's okay, Dad."

"You're so much like my mother," Dad went on

in that same weird voice. "Did I ever tell you that? She never liked me much, never liked my friends, never wanted me to be a cop, either. It wasn't *intellectual* enough for her." He stared at the angel. "But a cop is all I ever wanted to be." He chuckled. "S'funny. Now I'm not really a cop anymore. I guess she got her way after all."

"Dad?" My voice sounded so puny.

He turned the angel over in his hands. "I wanted her to be proud of me so bad. She never said she was. And now she never will."

Silence.

"You can yell at me," I offered. "Or ground me."

More silence. Terrible silence. Then his eerie voice again.

"I always thought: 'Deeton, if you play by the rules, you'll do okay. You might not be the best or the brightest, but you'll do okay.' That's a joke, huh?"

Dad picked up the gold satin football again, tossed it into the air, and caught it.

"But the funny thing," he went on, "the really funny thing is, that all of it, Meemaw, losing out to Jordan, even knowing I might never be a real cop again, just some old guy popping pain pills, it's all nothing — *nothing* — compared to this. I had a son. He *was* the best and the brightest. I was a good father. And I would give my life for just one more day with him."

Then I saw the outline of my father's body bend over, and heard the sound of his wracking sobs.

Fly, fly away! I told myself.

Stupid me. I couldn't fly.

So instead I wrapped my arms around myself, to keep from shattering into a million pieces, and concentrated on breathing; in, out, in, out.

So I would stay alive.

11

I sat on my bed, my backpack next to me, and by the early morning light I read over the letter I'd just written to my parents. My plan was to leave the letter on my dresser. They would have no reason to look there until much later, when they began to worry that I hadn't come home.

> Dear Mom and Dad,
> By the time you read this, I will be gone. I wanted you to know why, so you won't think it's your fault. Sometimes at night, when I can't sleep, I sit under my window and look up at the stars. When I was little, Meemaw taught me the name of stars. My favorite is Betelgeuse, in Orion. It glows bright red, and it's 527 light-years from Earth. That means the bright red light of Betelgeuse I see now actually left there 527 years ago. But the amazing thing is, if Betelgeuse died tonight, its light would still shine on Earth for another 527 years. I wish it was like that

when someone you love dies, but it isn't. Their light goes out right away, and you can't fool yourself into thinking that maybe they still exist, like you can with a star. But if a person's heart is still beating, then their light is still shining. That's why I have to find David's heart. I lied when I told everyone that I don't know what happened. The truth is, it's my fault that David ran into the street that night. You should not have to live in the same house with your son's murderer, so

That's where I had stopped writing. I put the pen to the paper, to finish.

So this is why I am never coming home again, is what I would write.

I tried. But I couldn't.

And I couldn't leave the letter for them, either, because then they would hate me almost as much as I hated myself.

My father was right. I was the biggest coward in the world.

I tore the letter into teeny, tiny pieces and stuffed them into my backpack.

It was time to go.

"Ticket, please," the bus driver held out his hand.

I handed him my ticket to Miami. So did Sam. He was wearing his zebra-striped sunglasses.

"You kids traveling alone?"

"Our mom's out there," Sam said vaguely, putting his arm around my shoulders. "Sis and I are going to visit Granny."

The bus driver craned his neck, searching for "Mom."

A crazy lady with no teeth stuck her head out the door of the depot, and spoke to a person who wasn't there.

"Bye, Mom!" Sam yelled, waving at her.

Startled, she focused on Sam, then grinned a toothless grin and waved back.

We walked toward the back of the bus. Sam stood on the armrest of a seat so he could reach the overhead rack. He shoved his backpack in. I handed him mine, which was so heavy he nearly dropped it before shoving it in, too.

"What happened to packing light?" he asked, as we slid into the seats below our luggage.

"Good morning, ladies and gentlemen, this bus is heading for Miami, Florida," the driver said over the public address system, as he maneuvered the bus away from the terminal. "For your convenience, you'll find a comfort station in the rear of the bus. We'll stop for meals every so often. Now sit back, relax, and enjoy the trip. And Merry Christmas."

"Congenial," Sam said, "though it would be sensitive if he used the ecumenical 'happy holidays' instead."

"We're really doing it," I whispered, my forehead pressed to the window. The bus headed south. There was no going back now.

"I suppose you realize that by late afternoon everyone will be looking for us," Sam said. "It won't be long before the cops interview the woman at the ticket window."

"Who says she'll remember us? And even if she does, she won't remember where we were going. It's the holidays. She sells a ton of tickets." I sat back, my body tense. "Did you bring food?"

Sam nodded.

"Me, too. An econo-sized jar of peanut butter and jelly swirled together. And a loaf of white bread."

"*That's* why your backpack is so heavy."

My hardcover copy of *The Member of the Wedding* — the novel Jayne had given me that terrible night, number twenty-eight on Meemaw's reading list — was in there, too. So was the journal Sam had given me, with the articles about David.

These are stupid things to carry when you're running away from home forever.

I didn't tell Sam any of that.

"Hello," the lady across the aisle said, smiling timidly. She looked about the same age as Bette, but she was dressed like a child, in pastel-pink ruffles. Her gray hair was held back by a girlish, stretchy, blue headband, and a small, blue, plastic-looking purse was clutched in her hands. She had a semi-wilted pink carnation pinned to the sweater draped over her shoulders, held there by a cheap, silver chain.

"Hi," Sam said, Mr. Friendly.

Friendly is not good when you're running away. Friendly can get you in big trouble. I shot him a warning look, but he paid no attention.

"Are you going home for Christmas?" she asked him.

"Lie," I hissed in his ear.

"Yep," Sam invented. "Home for Christmas. Home to Granny."

"Oh, my! What happened to your parents, if I might ask?"

"They're in the circus," Sam explained, nodding seriously. "They travel all the time. When we're not on the road with them, we stay with Granny."

"Well, goodness, that just sounds so exciting!"

"It's excellent," Sam said, so enthusiastically I half believed him myself. "I have my own act. But perhaps my reputation precedes me. The Great Samdini, greatest magician and escape artist in the world?" He hitched his finger at me. "She's my assistant."

"What an exciting life you lead! I'm Enid Manners." She held out her hand to Sam. "Please call me Enid."

"Sam —" he began, but I poked him hard in the ribs. This was no time to start giving out real names.

"— Monella!" he blurted out brightly. I guess it was the first thing that popped into his head.

Enid looked confused. "*Sal*monella, did you say? Isn't that a kind of food poisoning, dear?"

"Yes," Sam said, nodding seriously. "*So* confusing. Actually, my name is Sam-*Dean* Monella. "That's where I got my stage name — Sam*dini*. And this is my sister, Amanda-Bliss Monella."

"Pleased to meet you both," Enid said.

"Surely you've heard of our parents," Sam went on, "Patella and Rubella Monella, the Fabulous Flying Monellas?"

I was sure Enid would know Sam was goofing on her. After all, a patella is a bone in your leg, and rubella is a fancy word for measles.

Enid didn't even blink.

"I don't believe I have," Enid said seriously. "But I must confess, I haven't been getting out much. I've been caring for my mother. She just passed on."

I sat back. I didn't want to hear about death.

She and Sam chatted away. Sam told her outrageous whoppers about our life with the circus. I closed my eyes, I was so tired. Maybe it was the movement of the bus, or Sam sitting next to me, but I quickly fell asleep. The next thing I knew Sam was shaking my arm.

"Lemme sleep," I mumbled.

"It's lunchtime, Deed," Sam said. "We're in Indiana."

Groggily I opened my eyes. Except for Sam and me the bus was empty, parked in a bus depot. Across the street, I could see a diner.

I stretched and yawned. "How long did I sleep?"

"Five hours," Sam said. "Let's go in and eat."

"We've got food. We shouldn't spend money."

Sam got up. "Come on, I love diners. I'm thinking hamburger deluxe. And two pieces of pie. And a shake."

"We're eating peanut butter and jelly swirl." I got up and stood on the armrest, reaching for my backpack.

"Maybe *you* are. *I'm* eating in the diner."

I grabbed my backpack. The weight of it pulled me off balance and I landed on the floor of the bus with a thud.

"That's what you get for bringing an econo-sized jar of food," Sam said, helping me up. "You coming?"

"No," I said stubbornly.

"Okay, fine. I'll be sure to tell you how deelish it all was." He got off the bus.

I opened my pack and took out the huge jar of peanut butter and jelly. But though I tried with all my might, I couldn't open the jar. And the loaf of white bread was all squished.

I had been too nervous to eat any breakfast. My stomach growled, and I looked longingly out the window at the diner. I was such a weakling. No. I wouldn't give Sam the satisfaction of watching me slink in there.

I took *The Member of the Wedding* out of my backpack, opened it, bit into the squished bread, and began to read.

> *It happened that green and crazy summer when Frankie was twelve years old. This was the summer when for a long time she had not been a member. She belonged to no club and was a member of nothing in the world. Frankie had become an unjoined person who hung around doorways, and she was afraid.*

Too weird. It was exactly how I felt: a member of nothing in the world. An unjoined person. Afraid.

But whatever had made this girl Frankie feel so unjoined and afraid couldn't be as awful as what had made me feel that way. What I had done. What I could never undo.

An image of my father's silhouette the night before, bent over and sobbing, sprang into my mind.

Suddenly I couldn't eat the white bread anymore.

I lost myself in the book, so I wouldn't have to think. It worked. I didn't even realize when almost an hour had passed and people began to file back on the bus.

Enid tapped me on the shoulder. "Amanda-Bliss, is that all you ate, dear?"

I looked up. The open loaf of bread sat beside me.

"Oh, I ate . . . some other stuff, too," I said vaguely.

I saw Sam coming, so I scooted over next to the window.

"A burger, fries, and a chocolate shake," Sam said, plopping down next to me. "Superb."

"And don't forget the apple pie, Sam-Dean," Enid said.

"Right," Sam said, patting his stomach. "À la mode."

"Well, you're a growing boy," Enid said sweetly.

"It was nice of you to buy my lunch," Sam told her.

"My pleasure, young man. You were kind enough to keep me company."

Sam gave me a smug grin. "Yep, lunch was on Enid. She insisted. What could I do? So, how was the pea-bee swirl?"

"I couldn't get the stupid jar open," I mumbled.

The bus started moving. We were on the road again.

"Wow, Deed. You must be hungry."

"Did I ever mention how irritating you are, Sam?"

He dangled a small bag in front of my face that I hadn't noticed him carrying. The aroma coming from it was incredible. "Too irritating to eat this?"

I grabbed for the bag and opened it. Inside was a cheeseburger, my favorite.

"Sam-Dean thought you might be hungry," Enid said, as I ravenously bit into the cheeseburger.

"That was really thoughtful of Sam-Dean," I said, my mouth full.

I went back to the book. As I read Frankie's story, I *became* her. The countryside passed by as the afternoon light faded; I didn't notice. I was Frankie, and my beloved brother was getting married and moving far away. I wanted to go off with him and the bride, the three of us, together.

"They are the we of me," Frankie said. I mouthed the words to the steamed-up window of the bus.

A terrible ache closed my throat.

David had been the we of me. But then Jayne had become the we of him. If only I had opened my heart to her. If only I hadn't been so mean. If only I had —

Enid tapped me on the shoulder. I hadn't noticed that Sam had gotten up to use the "comfort station" and Enid had moved into his seat.

"I don't mean to interrupt, dear," she said hesitantly.

I put my finger in the book to mark my spot.

"I was wondering — you and your brother must travel a lot with the circus. I'm going to Nashville. I thought perhaps you could recommend a hotel that isn't too costly."

I shook my head no.

"Where is it that your grandmother lives, dear?"

"Near, uh . . . Disney World," I invented.

"Oh my, doesn't that sound exciting! Would you like to see a picture of where I live?"

No, I wanted to say. I don't care where you live. I want to read my book so I can stop thinking about my life.

But I didn't say that.

She reached into her little, plastic purse and pulled out a photo. "This is me and Mother," she said fondly. "Mrs. Cooper — she owns the rooming house — took this last June, on Mother's eighty-third birthday."

I looked at the photo. Enid was wearing the same frilly, pink dress she had on now. Her mother was a wrinkly old lady who looked like a zillion other wrinkly old ladies, with an oxygen tube in her nose, and a wrist corsage as ugly as the one Enid wore on her sweater.

Enid took the photo back, and stared at it. "It's so odd, being alone. I keep thinking of things to tell her."

She put the photo back in her purse. "If I'm frugal, I think I can stay in Nashville for three days."

Her eyes lit up. "I've listened to the Grand Ole Opry on the radio since I was a girl."

Suddenly, I felt ashamed. She was old and all alone and poor. The stupid-looking dress she had on must have been her best. That was why she wore it for her mother's birthday and for the bus trip. And here I just kept wishing she'd leave me alone. Sam was goofing on her. He'd gotten her to pay for his lunch and mine.

But her mother, who had been the we of her, was dead.

I knew exactly how that felt.

"Oh, hello, Sam-Dean, dear," Enid said, as Sam came back up the aisle. She stood up. "Amanda-Bliss and I were just having a lovely chat."

"Amanda-Bliss is very chatty." Sam slid into his seat.

Enid reached over and patted my hand. "You were very kind, dear." She sat back down across from us.

"So, Amanda-Bliss, dear," Sam whispered, "now that you bonded with ol' Enid, I bet she buys both of us dinner."

"Shut up, Sam," I said fiercely.

His eyebrows shot up. "What did I do?"

"Just . . . forget it." I started reading again. It was so much easier than feeling. Or trying to explain.

A while later I eased past Sam, who was sleeping, to use the "comfort station" at the rear of the bus. It had already become smelly and disgusting. When I came back, Enid was sleeping, too.

I looked down at her. Her plastic purse was wedged in next to her, holding everything she had in the world.

We had used Sam's money to buy our bus tickets, but I still had all of mine. I reached into the pocket of my denim jacket for my money purse. Then I took out a wad of singles and carefully slipped them into Enid's purse, right on top of the photo of the we of her, a wrinkled old lady with a tube in her nose, and on her wrist, that stupid, hopeful corsage of flowers.

12

"Clarksville, Tennessee," the bus driver announced over the PA system, as he pulled into the bus depot. "This will be a one-hour dinner stop. The bus will depart at nine o'clock. Change of driver. You all have a merry Christmas."

This time Sam didn't have to beg me to get off the bus. The night air was warm, so we didn't even take our jackets. I bent over and touched my toes, then I jumped up and down a few times. I was sick of that bus.

"Hey, Deed, look!"

Sam pointed across the street, where a winter carnival had been set up in a large parking lot. There was a merry-go-round, a Ferris wheel, all kinds of games of chance. A man dressed as Santa was selling Christmas trees. A big lit-up sign read CLARKSVILLE WINTER CARNIVAL. Music filled the air.

"Oh my," Enid said, her eyes shining. "Doesn't that look like fun?"

Sam pulled out his zebra-striped sunglasses and slipped them on, even though it was nighttime. "We are *so* over there already."

I turned to Enid. "Would you like to come with us?"

She looked across the street wistfully. "Oh, dear, I wouldn't want to be a bother."

"You're no bother," I insisted, hooking my arm through hers. "Come on."

I got into the ticket line and bought a bunch of ride tickets before Enid could pull out any money. Then the three of us went on the merry-go-round. Enid laughed out loud as she rode on a purple ceramic horse with daisies in its mane. It made me feel good.

After that, I bought us all cotton candy. Sam gobbled his and went back for a second. We walked by a line of little kids who were waiting to ride on Daisy the Docile Donkey. Past that were barkers hawking games of chance. I watched three guys who looked like they were in high school try to throw a football through a tire. They all failed. So I tried. The three boys laughed and nudged one another as I hoisted the football and eyed that round circle of air in the center of the tire.

David. All those hours we'd spent together in the backyard, when he showed me how to throw a football.

I let it fly.

Whoosh. The football sailed through like a rocket.

Sam and Enid clapped and whooped and hollered for me. I bowed and accepted my giant stuffed bunny from the vendor.

I skipped along, singing to my bunny, feeling so happy.

Until something hit me, like a fist in my gut.

David is dead. You killed him. And you're happy.

You are the most horrible person who ever lived.

A little girl in a dirty T-shirt was walking by, her hand held tight by her older sister.

"Would you like this bunny?" I asked her.

She pushed shyly into her sister's leg.

"She don't accept stuff from strangers," the older girl explained.

"I understand." I put the bunny on the ground in front of her. "The thing is, though, this bunny told me she belongs to you. So I'll just leave her here for you."

I walked away. Sam and Enid went with me, Sam looking back over his shoulder.

"Did she pick it up?" I asked.

"Affirmative," Sam said.

"What a nice girl you are, Amanda-Bliss," Enid said.

"Don't say that," I said sharply. "It isn't true."

We stood in front of a small stage, backed by

makeshift curtains. A muscular young guy with a blond crew cut, beady eyes, and no neck, was setting up some equipment — a microphone, a red, white, and blue trunk, a pair of handcuffs, and a sign that read AMAZIN' EDDIE: THE WORLD'S GREATEST TEEN ESCAPE ARTIST.

"What a coincidence, Sam-Dean," Enid said, "that young man does the same act you do with the circus."

Sam's eyes narrowed. He led us through the gathering crowd until we reached the front of Amazin' Eddie's stage, which hit both Sam and me about chest-high.

"Hi," Sam said, looking up at Amazin' Eddie through his zebra-striped sunglasses. Amazin' was setting up his microphone.

"Hey, kid." Amazin' barely glanced at him.

"So, wow, you're like the greatest teen escape artist in the world, huh?" Sam gushed.

Amazin' grunted.

"Gosh, Mr. Amazin', I had no idea that the greatest teen escape artist in the world was right here in Clarksville!"

Amazin' grunted again. He squatted down to check the red, white, and blue trunk.

More of a crowd gathered. We were pushed a little from behind against the lip of the stage.

"So, what's your big trick?" Sam asked, wide-eyed.

"Something this Houdini dude used to do," Amazin' said, now examining his handcuffs. "I do exactly the same trick he did, only better. I'm the only one in the world can do it. It's called Metamorphing."

Sam's smile got even brighter. "Gee, I heard it's called Metamor*phosis*."

"So you heard wrong."

Sam leaned way over the edge of the stage and reached for Amazin's handcuffs. "How do these work, Mr. Amazin'?"

"Get away from my stuff, ya little dweeb!" Amazin' yelled. He put the bottom of his sneaker on Sam's shoulder and pushed hard. Sam's zebra-striped sunglasses slipped off onto the stage. Sam fell down hard.

"Eddie Baylor, you should be ashamed of yourself!" a motherly woman admonished, as Enid and I gave Sam a hand up.

"It was an accident, ma'am," Amazin' said, flashing her a fake grin. He glanced at Sam's sunglasses, lying there on the stage. Then, as he walked over to move the microphone, he casually stepped on them, accidentally-on-purpose.

Crunch.

"Oops," Amazin' said. "Sorry, kid. An accident." He kicked the remains of the glasses off the stage, shot Sam a smug look, and disappeared behind the curtains.

"A true Neanderthal," Sam said, retrieving his

wrecked glasses. "Possibly even *pre*-Neanderthal. When exactly did mankind develop frontal lobes?"

"That boy has always been a bully," the motherly woman told us.

Enid patted Sam's back. "We'll find you some wonderful new sunglasses, Sam-Dean."

"The Great Samdini is always prepared," Sam said, pulling the James Bond-style black wraparounds out of his pocket and putting them on with a flourish.

The loud sound of a bugle fanfare filled the air, and Amazin' Eddie came out from behind the curtains. Now he had a blue satin jacket on over his T-shirt. He strode over to the microphone. The fanfare music stopped.

"Ladies and gentlemen, children of all ages, I am Amazin' Eddie, greatest teen escape artist in the world! Come one, come all. See me do a feat that has only been accomplished by the Great Houdini himself, Metamorphing!"

"Metamorphosis," Sam said under his breath.

I looked over at him. The crazy colored lights from the Ferris wheel made patterns on his face. I could tell by the set of his mouth that he was beyond furious.

"And now please welcome my assistant, the lovely Charlene!" Amazin' announced.

A pretty teenage girl, chewing bubble gum and wearing a red sequined leotard, came out from behind the curtain. A few people applauded.

"You are about to see me, Amazin' Eddie, assisted by the beautiful Charlene, do Houdini's world famous trick, Metamorphing."

"Metamorphosis," Sam muttered again, his jaw clenched even tighter.

"Handcuffed before your very eyes, I will escape from a padlocked trunk!"

"Can I get a volunteer from the audience?" Amazin' Eddie's eyes scanned the crowd. "How about you, sir?" he pointed to a burly, middle-aged man in the crowd. I checked my watch. We still had thirty minutes.

Amazin' had the man check his handcuffs and his trunk. He even had the man check inside his mouth, to make sure he didn't have a key hidden in there.

"Thank you, sir," Amazin' Eddie said, as the man returned to the crowd. "And now, folks, Metamorphing!"

Sam couldn't take it. *"Metamorphosis,* you Neanderthal!" he yelled.

Amazin' shot him a dangerous look.

Fast-paced music began to blare out of a tinny sound system. Charlene handcuffed Eddie, who got into the trunk. She locked the trunk and roped it shut. Then, swiftly, she brought out a screen and put it in front of the trunk.

The crowd buzzed with excitement while Charlene walked back and forth across the stage, posing like a game-show hostess on TV. She checked her watch dramatically, then called to the audience. "Say the magic words, y'all: 'Merry Christmas'!"

"Merry Christmas!" the crowd shouted, except for me and Sam. Caught up in the excitement, Enid shouted the loudest of all.

Amazin' pushed the screen back and held his arms over his head, the handcuffs dangling from one wrist. The trunk was still padlocked and roped shut.

"Thanks so much, folks," Amazin' said into the microphone. "And now, the lovely Charlene will pass amongst you with a hat. Just drop in what you can afford, folks. That's how we'll know that you appreciated our show."

"What did you think of his act, Sam-Dean?" Enid asked.

"He stinks," Sam muttered darkly. "*She* was supposed to end up locked inside the trunk. Plus *he* was only handcuffed, not tied in a sack. He could call himself *Bogus* Eddie."

When Charlene got to us, holding out a top hat that was already full of money, Sam dropped his wrecked zebra-striped sunglasses in. She shrugged and moved on.

I grabbed Sam's arm. "Let's go on the Ferris wheel."

He shook me off. "The Great Samdini is brooding. Go with Enid."

"Oh, dear, no," Enid said, "heights make my

head go all funny." She checked her watch. "We still have twenty minutes. What about if I go across the street to that restaurant and order the two of you cheeseburgers. That's your favorite, isn't it, Amanda-Bliss?"

"Thanks, but we're not hungry," I said quickly, since I didn't want her to spend her money or to discover the extra money I'd put in her purse. "Too much cotton candy. So we'll see you back on the bus."

She hesitated a moment. "I confess I was nervous about traveling alone. Sometimes the world is such a cold place. I just want to tell you both that you are two of the nicest young people I've ever met. And I am having a most wonderful time."

"Thanks," I said, dragging Sam toward the Ferris wheel.

"Sheesh, Deed, quit pulling on me," Sam said.

"Well, hurry up, then. I really want to ride the Ferris wheel and I don't want to miss the bus."

A bucktoothed guy took our tickets for the Ferris wheel. It was my favorite ride in the world.

"Why didn't you let Enid buy us cheeseburgers, anyway?" Sam asked, as we climbed into the rocking seats. "She wanted to do it."

"Just because." The attendant closed the safety bar.

Sam nodded. "Ah. It's *so* much clearer to me now."

The Ferris wheel started, and suddenly the world was at my feet. Below us was a quilt of crazy colored lights, above us was a blanket of stars.

"I never, ever want to get off," I yelled into the wind. "Let's stay on here forever."

"Forever and ever!" Sam yelled, holding his hands over his head.

The wind rushed past my face as we swooped and rose, swooped and rose again through the air. A whir of joy hit my stomach, just because I was alive, with Sam on a Ferris wheel. I looked up, searching the sky for Orion, for the steady red light of Betelgeuse.

"There! There it is! Betelgeuse!" I helped Sam to find it in the sky.

But then, too soon, it was over. The wheel had gone round and round, and though I had felt like I was flying, I had ended up in the exact same place. Nothing had changed. David was still dead. I was still a murderer. I had run away from home to find the kid who had gotten David's heart.

And I had no idea what I would say to him when I met him.

Or even if I really had the courage to meet him at all.

We were at the very top of the wheel. I looked up at the sky. Clouds had moved in. Betelgeuse was gone.

"Why is it that good things end so quickly and bad things seem to just go on and on?"

Sam shrugged. "Dunno." He stared up at the sky, too. "I feel almost tall up here."

Silence.

"When did you feel the very best about yourself, Deed?"

"I can't remember," I admitted.

He didn't look at me. "Remember in fourth grade when Henry Farmer called me Shrimp-boy for about the zillionth time? And I finally kicked him?"

"When he broke your nose?" I asked him. "*That's* when you felt the best about yourself? How come?"

"'Cuz it's the only time I wasn't a coward."

Our car swung slightly in the breeze. We weren't moving. I looked down below us. The attendant kept pressing the lever that ran the Ferris wheel, only nothing was happening.

"Uh, Sam, do you see what I see?"

He raised his sunglasses and looked down, too. Now a man who looked like a supervisor was hurrying over to the attendant. A crowd was starting to form, people were pointing toward us and the other cars.

The supervisor hit the lever. Nothing happened. He hit it again, harder. Nothing. The crowd grew larger.

The wind picked up. I shivered.

Sam looked at his watch. "The bus leaves in seven minutes."

"They won't leave without us. Enid won't let them."

Now two policemen hurried over to the supervisor. He waved his hands all around, explaining something to them. Seeing their police uniforms reminded me of my father.

I didn't want to think about my father.

One of the policeman pulled the lever for the wheel. Nothing happened. In the next car down, a little girl started to cry. A bigger girl comforted her.

Across the street, people boarded the bus. One woman stood there, looking toward the carnival. I figured it was Enid, worried. A new uniformed driver got on the bus.

And still, we hung there. And hung there.

"Three minutes," Sam said, looking at his watch again.

I cupped my hands around my mouth. "WE HAVE TO GET OFF OF HERE!" I yelled down. "WE HAVE TO GET ON A BUS!"

Sam looked at me. "In what fantasy is that helpful?"

We waited some more. Both of us knew it was past time for our bus to leave. I kept my eyes trained on it, as if I could will it not to leave without us.

"Attention, people on the Ferris wheel," one of the cops said into a PA system off his squad car, which he had pulled up to the Ferris wheel.

125

"There is a minor mechanical problem with the wheel. No need to worry, you're in no danger. We'll have you down in just a few minutes, folks. Just sit tight."

No, no, no. This couldn't be happening. My knuckles were white on the safety bar, my eyes glued to the bus.

Five minutes later, it pulled out of the bus depot.

I looked at Sam. "This is not good."

"Succinctly put."

We watched the bus grow smaller. "Our backpacks are on there," I said. "All our stuff. Everything."

My copy of The Member of the Wedding. *My journal with the articles about David pasted in it.*

A huge lump filled my throat. I willed myself not to cry. "Okay, we're not panicking. We've still got the rest of your money. We'll have to spend it on new bus tickets."

Sam's face got funny.

"Sam? You *do* have your money. Don't you?"

"Actually, I was afraid it might fall out of my pocket," he said, "so I put it —"

"— in the backpack," we said at the same time.

I felt the color drain out of my face.

Sam raised his palm to me. "Remain calm. We're not broke. We have your money."

I bit my lower lip. "I . . . kind of gave some of it

to Enid. Secretly. I kind of slipped it into her purse."

He stared at me as if I had grown horns.

"She's poor, okay? And she bought you lunch, anyway. And she's lonely. I didn't know we were going to lose all your money."

"How much did you give her, exactly?" he asked slowly.

"Exactly not much."

I reached into my pocket and pulled out my coin purse. It contained exactly six one-dollar bills. "I guess I didn't exactly count what I gave her."

At that moment, the Ferris wheel began to move. The crowd below, and the people stuck on the Ferris wheel, all cheered.

We were saved.

But we had no backpacks, no warm clothes, no food, and no bus tickets. It was nighttime. We were someplace called Clarksville, Tennessee. Our bus was on its way to Florida without us.

And we had exactly six dollars to our name.

13

We got off the Ferris wheel, walked to the nearest bench, and sat down to think. My teeth were chattering, more from fear than from the cold.

"Okay, we need to look at this logically," Sam said. "Enid knows we never got on the bus. She's going to make the driver call the police if she hasn't called them already."

"She'll tell the cops to look for the Monella kids." I wrapped my arms around myself for warmth.

"Only there *aren't* any Monella kids," Sam pointed out.

"They'll look through our backpacks. They'll find my journal. Our parents will have reported us missing —"

"So it won't be long before they put two and two together, and figure out that *we're* the wild and crazy Monella kids, and that we're in Clarksville, Tennessee," Sam concluded.

We stared at each other.

I pulled Sam up. "We can't hang around here, that's for sure."

We walked through the carnival. "Maybe we could hitchhike to Florida," I said, rubbing my hands together to warm them up.

"They write slasher movies about kids who hitchhike."

We walked past Daisy the Docile Donkey. A man who looked kind of like my father was helping his little girl onto Daisy's back. I looked away. We passed a hot dog stand, and I inhaled the aroma of cooking chili and onions. I swallowed hard and tried not to think about food.

Sam eyed a pay phone, next to the Port-o-Potties. I could tell what he was thinking.

"No way," I said.

"Choice A: We call our parents. Choice B: We starve, then freeze, then get arrested, then *they* call our —"

"Choice C: We're not giving up!" I insisted.

Sam pushed his hair off his face. "I'll call, Deed, you don't have to —"

"No!" I pushed him away from me. "I'm not quitting. So good-bye and good luck."

I turned around and started walking.

"Deed!"

I kept walking. Not that I had anywhere to go. Sam trotted up next to me.

"I thought you were giving up," I reminded him.

"Sorry, I had a temporary moment of sanity.

But now that I'm *in*sane again," he held out his arms, "here I am."

We walked silently, heading nowhere. Somehow we found ourselves right near Amazin' Eddie's stage again. An audience was gathering for the next show.

"I wish I really was in the circus," Sam said darkly, as he eyed Amazin' setting up his microphone. "I could show the world how bogus Amazin' really is."

"Forget about him, Sam. Let's go. We've got to figure out a plan to —"

"Shhh," Sam hissed. His eyes were glued to the stage as the fanfare music began.

"Ladies and gentlemen, children of all ages, I am Amazin' Eddie, greatest teen escape artist in the world!"

"Sam —"

"Shhh!" He didn't even turn to look at me.

I groaned. Fine. Great. It was getting really late, we were in big trouble, but Sam was too busy watching Amazin' do his act to care.

Sam shook his head with disgust. "Look at these people, worshipping this fake! Houdini must be turning over in his grave."

"Sam —"

"I'll have to discuss it with the Great One later," Sam went on, his eyes following Amazin's every move, as he went through his act again.

I felt like screaming. So what if Amazin' was a

cheat and a bully and he was making lots of money ripping people off by doing only part of Metamorphosis? The cops were probably looking for us, we had six dollars, and —

Something clicked, and my brain rewound like a videotape. That bully Amazin' was making lots of money doing only half of Metamorphosis. And he *claimed* he was the only one who could do it.

Only he wasn't.

Sam could do it.

"The lovely Charlene will pass amongst you with a hat. Just give what you can, folks," Amazin' was saying into the microphone.

I didn't stop to think. I just opened my mouth, and this voice came out.

"Hey, Eddie!" I yelled up to him. "My friend here says your act stinks like puke!"

"I'm dead," Sam said.

The crowd murmured their surprise. People turned to look. Amazin's beady eyes searched for the owner of the voice. They lit on me.

"Yeah, I said it!" I yelled up to Amazin'. "And I meant it, too."

"Correction," Sam said. "We are *both* dead. And you have lost your mind."

"I know what I'm doing," I insisted, pushing to the front of the crowd. Behind me, Sam muttered darkly.

Amazin' looked down at me. "Did you say something, little girl? Or is it little *boy*?" He chuckled at his pathetic attempt at humor. The crowd whispered and stared, waiting to see what would happen.

I looked Amazin' dead in the eye. "I *said* you should call yourself Stinky Eddie."

He crouched down so only Sam and I would be able to hear him. "If you're not outta my face by the time I count three, I'm gonna pulverize your friend the midget."

I sneered at him. "You don't scare us. Does he, Sam?"

"Yes, actually," Sam replied.

"One," Amazin' counted. "Two . . ."

"This might be a good time to *leave*, Deed." Sam pulled on my arm, dragging me away.

"Quit pulling on me, Sam, I have a plan to —"

"*Adios*, Shrimp-boy!" Amazin' called.

Sam stopped in his tracks. He didn't turn around.

Shrimp-boy. How is it that bullies all over the country end up using the same stupid insults? What is it, some kind of franchise operation? And just how long are you supposed to take it, before you fight back?

I turned around. "Hey, Amazing-Stinky Eddie!" I called. "M-My friend here can d-do your trick better than you c-can!"

To my utter mortification, my stutter had returned.

Amazin' laughed in a nasty way. "C-Can n-not!" he singsonged in a high falsetto, imitating my stutter.

A few kids snickered, just like at home.

I took a deep breath. I would not stutter. I would not stutter. I would slow down and I would not stutter.

"Can, too!" I yelled back, my words measured.

No stutter. The crowd buzzed a little, on hearing my challenge.

"Let's just go, Deed," Sam said, pulling my arm again.

"I'll bet you fifty bucks he can!" I called.

Sam pretended to hang himself with an imaginary rope. Amazin' laughed, like we were a big joke.

"Afraid to take a bet off a little kid?" I called, taunting him.

"I never seen you back down before, Eddie!" a guy in the crowd said, laughing.

"Maybe the kid can do it," someone else said.

"Yeah, Stinky Eddie," I called, "maybe he can!"

Eddie's little pig-eyes got even smaller. "If your buddy wants to make a pint-sized jackass out of himself, it's no skin off my nose. It's a bet."

"Show us your money, Eddie!" a guy crowed, his voice teasing. "Maybe you ain't got none!"

"Maybe the brat ain't got none," Eddie shot back. "So after he loses, I'll just have to kick his butt fifty-bucks worth."

I put my hands on my hips. "Ha! *He's* gonna kick *your* butt!"

"Suicidal," Sam said. "Adjective. Destructive to one's own life. Good-bye."

I grabbed the hem of his T-shirt before he could make his escape. "Don't you get it? This is brilliant! You do the trick, he looks like a fool when a little kid does the trick better than him — I know your time is faster than his — people fill the hat with money, we're on the next bus!"

Sam leaned close. "Two minor points. The Great Samdini has never actually done Metamorphosis in *public*."

"You can do it, Sam. I know you can."

"Also, the real Metamorphosis takes two, remember?"

My stomach turned over. Somehow I had managed to forget all about that.

"You d-do it alone, like he d-did."

"If I do it alone, it isn't really Metamorphosis, which would make me as big a fake as he is," Sam insisted. "Forget it."

"Hey, baby brats!" Amazin' jeered. "Chicken out?"

Sam and I locked eyes. The crowd waited.

"Deed?" Sam asked.

There were only two ways to go — back to where we had been, or forward into the scary unknown. Backward was safe. But forward was toward David's heart.

I took a deep breath.

"Let's do it," I said.

14

We pulled ourselves up onto the stage.

"Go say something into the microphone while I check out his stuff again," Sam told me.

I looked out at the crowd, frozen to the spot. Sam stabbed his finger toward the microphone.

I walked over to it on Jell-O legs. Amazin' stared at me, his folded arms the size of two Goodyear blimps.

"Hello," I croaked, my mouth at least six inches below the microphone. "I'd l-like to introduce —"

"Louder!" someone yelled.

Amazin' grabbed the microphone. "Hey, folks, that squirt over there bet me he can do my act better than I can!"

A bunch of people laughed.

"Well, heck, folks, I couldn't turn the little feller down, could I? It might injure his manhood!"

Some people tsked their disapproval at Amazin's meanness, but others just laughed. Sam was busy examining the handcuffs. My face burned with anger and embarrassment.

"Hey, if any of you want to place a friendly wager on Tiny Tim over there, I got ya covered!" Amazin' crowed.

"I'll bet on you, Eddie," a girl yelled.

Amazin's eyes scanned the crowd, lighting on a guy in a University of Tennessee jacket. "Hey, Billy, hold the bets until I win, buddy?"

"Sure thing," Billy said. He pulled a bill out of his wallet. "But my money's on the kid. For ten."

The crowd ooed their surprise.

"Mine, too," another guy said, handing some money to Billy. "You good for this, Eddie?"

Eddie scowled. "I got it covered. I just hate to see you throwing your money away."

More and more people bet, a lot of them on Sam, which made Amazin' madder and madder.

"I haven't got all night, kid," Amazin' snapped irritably. "Let's see your dumb little show."

Sam stopped examining the props. "Fine. As soon as I see dumb *big* you leave the stage."

The crowd laughed. Amazin' jumped down into the crowd.

"Everything okay?" I whispered to Sam.

"K-O."

"W-What if I can't p-pick the lock? Or g-get in the b-box, Sam?"

He smiled at me. "I believe in you, Deed."

I nodded, too scared to speak.

Sam went to the microphone. He stood on his tiptoes, then finally bent it down level with his mouth. "Ladies and gentlemen," his voice boomed, "I am the Great Samdini! Pay no attention to those who *pretend* to do the Great Houdini's most famous escape. I, the Great Samdini, and my assistant — I mean my *partner* — the one and only Dee Dee Demento, will show you how it's really done! And now we present . . . the *real* Metamorphosis!"

I bent down and punched the on button on the tape player. Amazin's tinny music filled the air. Sam opened the trunk and stepped inside. I clicked the handcuffs on him. He lay down, curled up.

"Deed!" he called as I was about to close the lid.

"What?"

"Remember we haven't got a lock pick for the handcuffs. You have to use a bobby pin." He pointed to my hair.

It is *much* harder to pick a lock with a bobby pin. I closed the lid and locked the padlock. Then, with every eye on me, I wound the ropes tightly around the trunk.

Now what? The screen! I dragged it in front of the trunk, then I clapped my hands three times, just the way Houdini and his wife used to do. I ran behind the screen, to find that Sam had already escaped. Quickly I reached for the bobby pin in my hair to pick his handcuffs. I jiggled the bobby pin in the lock, and it fell apart like butter.

Now was the moment.

I had to climb in the box.

I stared at Sam, a single rivulet of sweat running down my forehead.

His eyes held mine. He nodded.

I got into the trunk.

It was so dark. And tiny.

I couldn't breath.

You'll be out in just a second, I told myself. *Sam is running around the screen now. He'll clap his hands three times. Then he'll move the screen, he'll remove the ropes and unlock the padlock, and you'll get out. Just listen for him to clap his hands.*

"Hey, I bet the little kid's ticklish!" I heard Amazin' hoot to Sam from the other side of the screen.

"Get your hands off me!" I heard Sam yell back.

What was happening? Had Amazin' jumped up onstage to wreck Sam's trick? But if Sam didn't finish the act, I'd never get out of the trunk!

No. That was stupid. *Of course* I'd get out.

"Hey, Eddie, take the handcuffs off the kid!" I heard someone yell.

My heart swelled with panic.

"Nah, he's such a little Houdini, let's see him do it himself!" Amazin' hooted.

Amazin' had handcuffed Sam.

Sam can pick the handcuffs with a bobby pin, I reminded myself.

And then I remembered.

He didn't have the bobby pin.

Because I had stuck it back in my hair.

The panic began with a spark at the back of my neck. It caught, spreading like wildfire, blanketing me in sweat. Louder and louder, my heart beat, a deafening pounding in my ears. *Breathe!* I ordered myself. *Keep breathing! In, out, in, out . . .*

I *had* to get out, or I would die. There was a way for me to do it, too. But if I got out, the trick would be ruined.

Which would mean no one would give us any money.

Which would mean I'd never get to my brother's heart.

I gulped hard, tasting my own sweat as it ran salty into my mouth.

I couldn't give up. I *wouldn't.*

Now it seemed the trunk was my coffin, just like David's coffin, and I couldn't breath, I was drowning, sucking for air that didn't exist, buried alive as punishment for the awful, terrible thing I had done.

Breathe, I ordered myself. *In, out, in, out —*

Suddenly, there was light. Air gushed at me, I drank it in. Sam's hands reached for me, helping me out of the trunk. I stumbled out on shaky legs, still handcuffed.

The crowd cheered, whistled, stomped their feet. Sam spun me around and, our backs to the audience, he quickly pulled the bobby pin from my hair, worked it into the handcuffs, and they fell apart, dangling from my wrist.

We turned back to the audience, who clapped and whistled as we bowed together.

I'm a helium balloon, I thought crazily, as I grinned ear to ear. *A bright red helium balloon. I could fly to the sun, to the stars. I did it!*

"Did Amazin' cuff you?"

"Affirmative."

"So how did you get the cuffs off? I had the bobby pin!"

"Oh, ye of little faith," Sam said, as we bowed again.

He lifted his T-shirt. And there were six bobby pins stuck to his stomach under a strip of masking tape.

"A true professional keeps extra bobby pins on him for emergencies at all times," Sam explained, as we took yet another bow.

"Looks like you better pay the kids fifty big ones!" Billy hooted to Amazin'. "And then you can settle up with all of us!"

Clearly Amazin' didn't want to pay us, but with everyone watching, he didn't have a choice. Red-faced, he counted out fifty dollars and handed it to Sam. Then he began to pay off all the people who had bet against him.

"Quick, pass the hat, Deed!" Sam told me.

I grabbed the top hat, which lay onstage, and jumped down into the crowd. People began stuffing bills into it, patting me on the back, telling me how terrific Sam and I had been.

Amazin' was still paying off his debts, looking more furious by the second. Sam was in the middle of a crowd of admirers.

"You kids were really something!" a man told him. "I won ten bucks off Eddie, so this is for you." He handed Sam five dollars.

"It was a true pleasure to watch a little feller like you whup that bully, fair and square," another man said, handing Sam more money.

More and more people who had bet against Eddie handed Sam money, while others filled up my hat. Sam stuffed money into all of his pockets, grinning hugely.

Someone tugged on my sleeves. I looked down. A little girl with eyes as big as Frisbees looked up at me, a red helium balloon in one hand, a scrap of paper and a pencil stub in the other.

"I love your balloon," I told her.

"Thanks," she said shyly. "Can I have your autograph, Miss?"

Me? Sign an *autograph*?

Yes, me. Dee Dee Demento. It had a certain ring to it. I reached for the pencil and started to sign my name.

"Those kids over there!" I heard Amazin' yell. "They stole my money from the last show!"

I looked up. Amazin' had two cops with him. The cops started for us.

I grabbed Sam. "Run!"

We took off, pushing through what was left of the crowd, darting around people to make our getaway. The cops and Amazin' were gaining on us.

"This way!" I yelled, tugging Sam.

We sprinted toward a thicket of bushes, plowing through them, sticker branches scratching our faces.

"We didn't steal his money!" I said, panting, as we ran out onto the sidewalk, turned left, and skirted behind a building. We both stopped, breathing hard.

"I'm sure the police will be delighted to hear that," Sam said between pants, "after they ask us for ID."

"And then we're ruined," I concluded, as I stuffed the money from the hat into every pocket I had.

At any moment I expected to hear the cops, snarling dogs, even helicopters, like in prison escape movies. What if the cops had found out who we really were? What if no one in the crowd defended us?

I was so scared.

It's just so easy to bring down a helium balloon. One prick, it's over.

Go home, a voice in my head told me. *Just give up.*

And do what? another voice inside me asked. *Bury yourself in the backyard with the baby bird?*

I looked over at Sam for an answer, only to find that he was looking at me the same way.

All right, then.

I would *pretend* myself right through the fear.

"Let me see what I can see," I told Sam. I rounded the corner, hugging my body to the building, then peeked around the other side. Amazin' was gone, but the two cops were standing not twenty feet from me.

"They ran out of the carnival," the taller cop said into his walkie-talkie. "Just a couple of local kids, I reckon, over. . . . Say what? . . . Eddie lost a bet to them, that's all? . . . Yeah, I copy. That's a big ten-four. We're heading back. Over and out."

They turned around and walked away. I waited, to make sure they were really gone. Then I hurried back to Sam.

"Remember we get one phone call," Sam said, his teeth chattering now that he'd cooled down. "And we don't say anything until we talk to our lawyer."

I told him what I'd heard.

"Astonishing," Sam said. "They still don't know we're runaways. Adults can be amazingly inefficient. I suggest we get on the next bus. And wherever we end up, we'll catch another one to Miami."

We skirted the carnival, which was beginning to shut down, and made our way back to the bus depot. But as we approached, there were two completely different policemen standing just inside the front doors.

I pulled Sam back. "If they weren't looking for us before, they are now," I whispered. "No way can we get on a bus."

The cops spoke to each other, then one began to walk toward the door. We sprinted back over to the carnival.

Things were shutting down now. The games of chance were closed. Daisy the Docile Donkey was being led into a trailer hitched to a small truck. No music. No colored lights. Everything seemed to signal "the end."

Maybe it *was* the end. I was so tired.

I sat on a bench. "Now what?" My teeth chattered.

Sam sat next to me, shivering. "Being a fugitive is highly overrated." He closed his eyes.

A woman in jeans walked over to the man who had just led the donkey into the trailer. "Y'all heading out?"

The man nodded. "Thought I might get to Valdosta, Georgia, by morning. Got a gig there tomorrow afternoon."

"Step over here and I'll pay you," the woman said.

He walked with her to a nearby bench, where they sat and did business.

I looked at Sam. His eyes were still closed. I nudged him hard. "Sam!"

He opened his eyes.

"I think I've got a plan."

"Thrilling."

Keeping my eye on the man and woman on the bench, I grabbed Sam's hand and we snuck toward the donkey trailer. Daisy the Docile Donkey was tethered inside. She stared at us. The door hadn't been shut yet.

"Get in," I told Sam.

"You're not serious."

The woman stood up. So did the man. They shook hands. The man was walking toward us.

I pushed Sam into Daisy's trailer. We scrambled to the back, burying ourselves under the smelly hay, as far from Daisy as we could get, which wasn't very far.

"Okay, Daisy-girl, we're hitting the road," the man said, as he slammed the door of the trailer shut.

Slowly, I peeked out of the straw. I spit some out of my mouth. Sam's head peeked up, too.

Odd slants of light seeped in through the boards of the door. The truck started up. Daisy whisked her tail practically in our faces.

We were both too petrified to speak or to move.

The trailer pulled out of the fair, and onto the streets of Clarksville.

"Nice Daisy," I crooned, my voice shaking with fear. "Sweet Daisy."

We waited. Daisy's tail swished again. She didn't seem to mind us.

"This might work," Sam said cautiously.

I relaxed a little. We traveled in silence for another five minutes. Daisy was as docile as her name.

"This is most excellent," Sam decided, as we both relaxed some more.

"We're going to some place called Valdosta."

"Geography was never my strong suit." Sam yawned. He closed his eyes.

"It's in Georgia, somewhere." I rubbed my arms. "No one will be looking for us in Georgia."

Sam's eyes sprang open. "Did you ever tell Enid where we're going?"

I thought a minute. "I think I said that Granny lives near Disney World."

"Disney World?"

I nodded. "I guess it was stupid, but —"

"Deed, you are a genius!"

"I am?"

"It's so perfect!" he chortled. "Don't you see, that's where everyone's going to look for us! Two kids, best friends, one is unbelievably depressed, so they use their piggybank money and Hanukkah *gelt* to take a bus from Wisconsin to . . . Disney World!"

I made a face. "Who'd believe that?"

"Adults," Sam said. "It's how their minds work."

We traveled in silence for a while.

"Deed?"

146

"Hmm?"

"Remember what I told you on the Ferris wheel? About feeling like a coward?"

"Uh-huh."

"I don't feel like such a coward anymore."

I could almost feel Sam smiling in the dark.

"Me, neither," I said. "I got in the box."

"I always knew you could, Deed."

"Yeah. But now *I* know I can."

The moving trailer began to lull me to sleep, despite how cold it was.

Sam's stomach growled. "You know, even that pea-bee swirl you had sounds good right about now."

Daisy's stomach made the same noise. She swished her tail again, harder, and kicked out a hind leg.

"Uh, donkeys don't eat people. Do they, Sam?"

"Only if they're really, really, hungry."

I eyed Daisy nervously. "Let's hope Daisy ate dinner, then."

Sam looked directly up at Daisy's hind end. "Deed," he said, "let's hope she didn't."

15

The first thing I noticed was the smell of donkey poop.

The second was how freezing I was. I opened my eyes, shivering. The trailer was slowing down, pulling off the interstate, and morning sunlight streamed in through the slats of the door. Daisy's tail whisked by my nose.

In spite of the disgusting scent of donkey, my stomach rumbled hungrily.

Sam was still asleep, wrapped up in a ball, his sunglasses half on and half off. I shook his arm.

"I'm-not-going-to-school-I-have-a-sore-throat-let-me-sleep-turn-up-the-heat-Mom," he said without opening his eyes. He curled into a tighter ball.

"Oh, Sa-am," I singsonged. "Inhale!"

He did. His eyes popped open as he gagged. He held his nose. "I see Daisy has spoken. Where are we?"

"I don't know." I looked at the opening in the trailer door. It was up high, so a horse could poke its head out. Docile Daisy wasn't quite tall enough to reach it.

"You think we can get out that hole?" I asked Sam.

"Need you ask the Great Samdini and Dee Dee Demento such a question?" Sam scoffed between shivers.

"Let's just say it helps that we're little and skinny." I looked up at Daisy. I knew that we had to get out of the trailer before Daisy's owner checked on her. From where I sat, she looked really, really big.

"Nice Daisy," I crooned, and began to slide my body along the wall toward the rear of the trailer.

"Nice, *stinky* Daisy," Sam added, sliding along the opposite wall.

Daisy made a noise and kicked a rear leg hard.

"Sheesh," Sam muttered, "that leg kicked the spot I just vacated."

"I think you insulted her." I inched farther along the wall, keeping my eye on Daisy's hooves.

Finally we both made it to the door, as the pickup truck and trailer slowed to a stop. There were a few two-by-fours nailed to the trailer door. With numb, freezing fingers I grabbed the lowest one, and began to climb. Sam was right behind me. Now that Daisy could see us, she didn't seem to like us much. She began to whinny, and kicked so hard the trailer shook.

I reached the opening, the trailer rocking from

Daisy's kicks, and slid my head out. I saw the owner of the truck head into the interstate highway rest area building. That was good — he wouldn't catch us. I scootched half of my body through.

I looked down and gulped. It was such a long drop.

I took a deep breath and, knees bent, I dropped. I landed in a squat, and toppled over onto my butt. Sam dropped, too.

We stood up, brushed each other off, and looked around. We were parked, surrounded by giant rigs, at a huge rest area, heading south on some interstate. At the other end of the parking lot was a restaurant called the Country Pantry and a place to get gas.

I stuck my hands inside my jean jacket. "I wonder what state we're in."

"A state of hunger," Sam said, shivering. He looked at his watch. "It's eight. Can you spell 'breakfast,' boys and girls?"

We sprinted over to the restaurant, and both went to the restrooms. I looked at my face in the mirror. I was filthy and my hair was a tangled mess, full of hay, sticking every which way out of my scrunchie. I washed my face and hands, and picked the hay out of my hair.

I sniffed, and made a face. I stunk of donkey. I spotted an aerosol can of lilac air freshener on a shelf above the sink. Quickly, I sprayed it all over myself.

"Good news," Sam said, when we met up outside the rest rooms. "There's a map on the wall and . . . you smell like lilacs."

"Air freshener," I told him. "Scent of lilacs beats scent of Daisy."

"Excellent point. Be right back."

I studied the map on the wall. He was back in sixty seconds, reeking of pine.

"We're in *southern* Georgia," I told him eagerly, pointing to the map on the wall. "Like as close to Florida as you can get without actually being in it already."

"I know."

I shivered. "Then why is it so cold?"

Sam shrugged. We walked into the Country Pantry restaurant. A waitress walked by with a full tray, got a whiff of our wearable room freshener, and made a face.

"I'm digesting my stomach lining," Sam said, heading for a table.

"Wait!" I pulled him back. Two state highway patrolmen were sitting in the front booth, eating breakfast. "They might be looking for us."

"Unlikely, Deed."

"Two kids, no adults, we could attract attention," I muttered, looking around. I pulled Sam out of the restaurant and toward the attached convenience store.

We bought three hot dogs apiece, paid for them, and gobbled them down on the spot. Nothing had

151

ever tasted so good in my entire life. The only warm clothes for sale were sweatshirts with Elvis's face silk-screened on the front, and the only size left was adult XXL. We bought two and put them on.

"Hey, nice," I said, looking down at myself. The sweatshirt hung to my calves, the sleeves practically hit the floor. Sam looked equally ridiculous. "We could fit Daisy in here with us."

Sam tried to roll the sleeves up to a manageable length. But they wouldn't stay rolled. "We could fit her *trailer* in here with us."

Sleeves hanging, we picked out a small backpack, then headed for the junk food aisle to load up: cupcakes, candy, chips, beef jerkies, and a huge box of chocolate candies called Goo-Goo Clusters. Sam was in heaven.

"Where you kids headin' with a backpack full of food?" the woman behind the counter asked between gum chews as she rang up our stuff.

"Camping!" I chirped. "With Mom and Dad. They're out in the car."

She took in our oversize Elvis sweatshirts, and looked doubtful. "During this cold spell? In that getup?"

"Elvis was the King, you know," Sam told her solemnly. "We collect everything that has his picture on it."

Next to the register was a pile of sunglasses. Elvis was growing out the corners of each pair, his hinged legs dancing above the lenses. A sign read: SALE: DANCING ELVIS SUNGLASSES $8.00. Sam picked up a pair and slapped his money down on the counter.

"Thank-yu, thank-yu very much," Sam told the clerk, as he did his best Elvis imitation and backed out the door.

Once we got outside, Sam eagerly reached into the backpack for the pink coconut and marshmallow Snoballs. He bit into one and closed his eyes blissfully. "Now this is what I call cuisine."

"We need to find out where the bus depot is." I chewed on a knuckle.

"We've undoubtedly been reported as runaways," Sam said, polishing off the first Snoball and reaching for the second. "They look for runaways at bus depots."

"Have you got a better idea?" I asked, as I stared out at the sea of trucks and parked cars.

Which gave *me* a better idea.

"What if one of these trucks is going to Florida?" I asked slowly. "We could check the license plates."

"True. On this side of the interstate, if the plates are from up north, odds are the driver is heading south."

"Well, we can't very well ask where he's going or ask for a ride. They'll just take us to the cops." I kicked the back of my sneaker against the building in frustration. "And we can't even sneak into the back. It'll be locked."

Sam sighed. "Deed, Deed, Deed. Who am I?"

The light dawned.

"The Great Samdini," I said, grinning, "who can pick any lock, anytime, anyplace, anywhere."

He lifted the massive Elvis sweatshirt and flashed the row of bobby pins taped to his stomach. "Shall we?"

I checked the plates on one row of trucks, Sam checked another. He started on the next row.

"Bingo!" he called.

I hurried over. He was standing by a huge truck that said GREAT NORTHERN U-MOVE-IT across the side. "The plates are perfect," he pointed out. "He's from Minnesota, and he's got an open map of Florida on the front seat. Be on the lookout while I get us inside."

"Do it fast," I said over my shoulder. "I think this is breaking and entering."

"A harmless felony for an excellent cause." He took off his Elvis sunglasses and reached for a bobby pin.

I kept my eyes glued to the restaurant and the convenience store while Sam picked the lock. Every time someone came out, I jumped, sure they were going to come catch us.

"Hurry up!" I called nervously.

"A true *artiste* can't be rushed in his work," Sam said, his eyes closed as he fiddled the bobby pin inside the lock.

"He can if it keeps him from going to jail."

"Just a little more, gotta feel for the catch, and . . . got it!" Sam cried. He held the lock in the air, dangling off one finger. "Do I rule, or what?"

Together we opened the huge, yawning back doors of the truck. It was filled with boxes and furniture covered in drop cloths. I threw our backpack in, then we scrambled in after it. As soon as we slammed the door again, it was so dark I couldn't see my hand in front of my face.

"This is creepy," I whispered. I felt something brush against my leg, and I shuddered. "There wouldn't be anything like rats in here. Would there?"

"Nah." Sam waited a beat. "*Snakes*, maybe."

"Very funny." I felt around with my hands like a blind person, edging along until I touched something soft and squishy. "Hey, I found a couch!" I sat down. It was very comfy. I lay down. "Wow, this is great."

"I think I just hit a chair," Sam said. "It feels like one of those big, soft ones."

"I feel like I could sleep for about a year." I snuggled down into the couch.

"Don't fall asleep until the truck's moving," Sam cautioned. "If someone notices the lock is open they'll look in here; we have to be ready to hide."

I knew he was right, but it was so dark and so much more comfortable than Daisy's trailer, and I was so tired, that I could feel myself nodding off.

I awoke with a start when I realized the truck was moving. "Sam!"

"We're moving, I know." His voice came from somewhere in the dark.

"Maybe we just got incredibly lucky and this guy is going all the way to Miami."

"Or maybe we'll get incredibly *un*lucky and this guy is going to Disney World, which is crawling with cops carrying our photographs even as we speak." Sam yawned. "I wish I knew where we threw the backpack. I could go for a Goo-Goo Cluster."

I wiggled my fingers in front of my face. I couldn't see a thing. "When we get to Miami, we have to look up the Pawlings' address."

"I tried to tell you before, I got it off the Internet white pages. It was easy. His parents are doctors, and we had both of their first names."

"Thanks." I hesitated. "We *are* going to find him. It's really going to happen. Isn't it?"

Sam must have already fallen asleep, because the only reply was his snoring.

But I also heard that voice inside my head, the one that wouldn't shut up lately: *With every turn of the big wheels underneath you*, it said, *you're getting closer to David's heart.*

And then, the voice added something else. Something I didn't want to hear.

Closer to David's heart. But . . . then what?

Then . . . what?

16

"**W**inston Pawling is rich," I said, my voice flat.

It was that evening, we were in Miami Beach, in a very ritzy neighborhood, standing across the street from Winston Pawling's house. It was all one level, painted pale pink, surrounded by lush gardens and tropical flowers. The wreaths on the double front doors were illuminated by a welcoming light. In each bedroom window, a single candle glowed. Through the large living room picture window, we could see a huge Christmas tree.

I thought about my house — dark, silent, lonely. Dad with the box of Christmas ornaments at his feet, but no tree to put them on.

It wasn't right.

"So what if he's rich?" Sam said, shrugging. "Both his parents are doctors. Doctors make *beaucoup* bucks."

I dropped the backpack on the sidewalk and sat on it. We had done it, made it all the way to Miami, all the way to the Pawlings' house. I was finally going to get what I wanted. But all I felt was mad.

Then . . . what?

I knew I should be happy. After all, we had completely lucked out. The moving van really had taken us to Fort Lauderdale. Of course, we hadn't known that when we jumped out of the van at yet another truck stop.

It was late afternoon. We bought a good map and studied it while we ate double cheeseburgers and fries in the restaurant.

It was Sam's idea to call a taxi out of the Yellow Pages and get them to take us right to the Pawlings' house. I had never taken a taxi in my life. But, as Sam pointed out in a very logical Sam-like fashion, we were nowhere near a bus line.

The taxi ride was *beaucoup* expensive, and we didn't know how long our money had to last. The Spanish-speaking driver, who had recently arrived from the Dominican Republic, wanted to practice his English on us. So he talked for forty-five minutes nonstop about the Marlins, Miami's baseball team.

He blessed us, half in English and half in Spanish, when we got out of the taxi. I guess it never occurred to him that we could be runaways.

And now, here we were. And this mad feeling was bubbling in my stomach.

I looked around. It was like Christmas on a different planet. A young couple walked by, their hands in the back pockets of each other's shorts. They both had Santa caps on their heads. A few houses down, someone had strung Christmas lights around a palm tree.

"Want to knock on the front door?" Sam asked me.

"No."

Sam sighed. "Scootch over."

I moved over on the backpack, which now held our mammoth Elvis sweatshirts, and Sam sat next to me. "So, what do you want to do, then?"

"Sit here." I drew my knees up to my chin and wrapped my arms around them. "How can people have Christmas when it's hot outside? It ruins everything."

"Dunno," Sam said. "I don't celebrate Christmas."

"You know what I mean." I scowled at the Pawlings' house. "How much do you think a house like that costs?"

"A lot. Listen, sitting here is not productive, Deed. The people who live in the house behind us are going to wonder what we're doing."

"It's a free country, okay?"

"K-O." He waited a moment. "You're scared, huh."

I didn't reply.

We just sat there. Then suddenly, he stood up. "All righty, then. I have a plan."

I looked up at him and raised my eyebrows.

159

"We turned off a main drag just a couple of blocks that way." He cocked his chin to the east. "We go find a store. We buy some jumbo-sized boxes of candy. We go ring the Pawlings' bell."

"As you would say, Sam, in what universe does that make sense?"

"This universe," he replied. "Come on, I'll explain while we're walking."

A half hour later, we were at the Pawlings' front door. In our backpack were three jumbo boxes of assorted chocolates.

I bit at a hangnail nervously. "Are you sure this is going to work?"

"Piece of cake," Sam replied. He rang the doorbell.

My heart pounded. What if a boy about twelve years old answered the door? It would be him, Winston. The only reason he would be there, living and breathing, would be because of my brother's heart.

No one answered the doorbell.

"No one's home, let's go," I said.

Sam grabbed the sleeve of my T-shirt to stop me from leaving, and rang again, longer this time.

Finally, so slowly, the door began to open. What if it was Winston? What would I say? What would I do?

But it wasn't Winston. Peering out at us curiously was a pleasant-faced black woman in jeans

160

and a ratty-looking sweatshirt. She had a scarf tied around her hair.

The maid.

My mom was working double shifts at the hospital to help pay the bills for Meemaw to lay in a bed at Happy Appleton Acres. If it wasn't for my father's back, he'd be moonlighting as a security guard, like he used to do. My parents couldn't afford to get me a computer. We were barely making ends meet.

The Pawlings were so rich that they had a maid.

The maid at my house was me.

"Can I help you?" the black woman asked.

"Good evening, ma'am," Sam said. He pulled the three jumbo boxes of chocolate out of the backpack. "We're selling candy door-to-door to raise money for our school. We have soft centers, nut-filled, or an assortment. Would you care to buy any?"

"Raise money for what?" the woman asked.

"Christmas," I blurted out. "I mean, for kids at our school who can't afford Christmas."

"What school is that?" the woman asked.

"Uh . . . Marlins Middle School," I invented. The baseball team was the first thing that popped into my head.

She frowned. "I've never heard of that school."

"It's new!" Sam explained brightly.

"Really new!" I added.

She tapped one finger against her lips. "You're

161

raising money for *Christmas*, you say? At a *public* school?"

"And Hanukkah," Sam added quickly. "And, uh . . . Kwanzaa, too. Yep, Marlins Middle takes pride in our cultural diversity. We celebrate our differences!"

She looked amused. "Well, you caught me in the middle of cleaning. I'm afraid no one here eats candy."

"Thanks, anyway," I said, trying to peer around her, into the house. All I could see was a big hallway with a gleaming slate-gray tile floor, and some plants.

"Good luck with your sale," the woman said. "And happy holidays, kids."

She shut the door.

We walked back across the street and sat down.

"I can't believe they have a maid," I said angrily.

"'Housekeeper' is the politically correct term," Sam said, opening a box of chocolates.

"We bought all that candy for nothing," I fumed. "We didn't get inside, and we didn't get to see Winston."

"Mmmm, caramel center," Sam said chewing happily. "If Goo-Goo Clusters are a ten, this is a serious eight."

I reached for a chocolate. "What if he's obnoxious?"

"Who?"

"You know who." I ate the chocolate and

162

reached for another. "What if it turns out he's a spoiled rich brat or a big stupid bully like Henry Farmer?"

Sam reached for another chocolate. "It's not something we have any control over, Deed."

"But it wouldn't be right," I insisted, "for a horrible person to be alive when David is . . ."

I didn't finish the sentence. But, of course, Sam knew.

He polished off another chocolate, stood up, and hauled me up, too. "All of this will look better in the A.M."

"How do you know?"

"I don't," Sam allowed. "But it's one of those stupid things adults always say, so I thought I'd try it out."

We started down the street.

"Are we wandering aimlessly?" I asked Sam.

"The answer to the final *Jeopardy* question is: On the beach," Sam said, doing his best imitation of a game-show host. "For five bazillion simoleons, Dee Dee Deeton, what is the question?"

"Where is sand?"

Sam made the rude sound of a loud buzzer. "Ohhhh, sorry! The correct question was: 'Where are we going to sleep tonight?'"

"Can't we get arrested for sleeping on the beach?"

"Only if we get caught."

I shifted the weight of the backpack. "Where is the beach, anyway?"

"We passed it in the taxi. If we keep walking east, we're bound to hit it."

We walked down the middle of the street in silence. I could already smell the ocean, and, as we got closer, I heard the sound of waves breaking.

"Yo, behind you!" A voice called.

We turned around. A skinny guy on a skateboard was zooming right at us. We jumped away just in time, as he whizzed by.

"Have a good one!" he called to us over his shoulder.

Up ahead, the street ended in a small park area, with wooden benches. I could see the kid who had passed us on the skateboard up there, doing tricks. When we got to the benches, he saluted us, then zoomed off.

I took off my backpack, and read the sign: NO CAMPING! NO ALCOHOLIC BEVERAGES! BEACH CLOSED AFTER 10 P.M.! VIOLATORS WILL BE PROSECUTED!

"Hmmmm, *beaucoup* exclamation points," Sam mused. "Not very HOSPITABLE!"

I plopped down on one of the wooden benches. "Now what?"

Sam brushed his hair off his face. "Possibly the overkill sign means that the cops don't actually patrol the beach. They hope the sign will scare everyone away."

I lay down on the bench, my knees up. "We can't take a chance. It says 'Violators will be prosecuted!'"

"They mean it, too," someone who was not Sam said.

I sat up. The kid on the skateboard was behind us, doing tricks.

"Cops around here haul you in fast, man," the kid said, standing on one edge of the skateboard until it tipped. Then he spun it around and jumped back on the other side. "I seen it happen to my buds. Bad news, man."

As he did more tricks, I looked him over. He wasn't too much older than us, maybe fifteen. His messy blond hair was mostly hidden under a red bandanna tied gypsy-style over his forehead. He wore super-baggy shorts that hung past his knees, and a T-shirt with Bob Marley on it. Sam's parents had returned from a trip to Jamaica with all these Bob Marley tapes. He was this great Jamaican reggae singer who had died young from a brain tumor.

"You guys need a place to crash?" he asked us.

"No," I said, at the same time as Sam said "yes."

The kid laughed and weaved his skateboard in and out of the benches. "Yo, first rule of the road, dudes, you gotta get your story straight. So which is it?"

"We might," I said cautiously.

"You wanna come with me, I'll show you where

165

a bunch of us crash, cops don't bother you there." He stopped his board in front of me.

"I'm Marley." He held out his hand to me. "It used to be Michael in a former life."

"What former life?" I asked, shaking his hand.

"Perrysburg, Ohio, man," Marley said ruefully. "Small town, small minds."

"I'm Amanda-Bliss," I told him. Weirdly, saying that was starting to feel normal. "That's my brother, Sam-Dean."

"*Twin* brother," Sam said, shaking Marley's hand.

Marley stepped on one end of his board and tipped it. "So, you coming with or not?"

Sam and I looked at each other. "With." I decided.

"Cool." He picked up his board.

The three of us walked down the beach, sand crunching under our sneakers.

"So how come the police don't bother you at this place on the beach where we're going?" Sam asked.

"Easy, man," Marley said, grinning. "It's haunted."

17

"**H**aunted?" Sam echoed.

"Who knows, man? Some runaway kid got killed there a few years back," Marley explained. "Skaters who've been around say his spirit protects us. Anyway, it's right by this party section of Miami Beach. The cops are too busy arresting drunks and druggies to bother with us."

As we walked, Marley told us his story. He was fourteen. His mom left a long time ago, his dad was some kind of business executive who was never home, and his new stepmom hated his guts.

He'd hitchhiked to Miami three weeks ago because he'd seen a feature on MTV about skateboarders who'd come here. He'd connected with other skaters right away. Now he called it home. When the skaters needed money, they panhandled and shared what they took in.

"Skaters are my people," Marley said. "We're family."

Family. Something I didn't have anymore.

After walking in silence for a while, we came to a giant wooden fishing pier that jutted out into the ocean.

"Welcome home," Marley said.

I looked around. I didn't see anybody. "Where?"

He cocked his head toward the pier. "Come on."

Built into the understructure of the pier along-side of the huge support pilings was a ladder, which Marley began to climb. Sam and I followed him. The ladder led to a wooden base level of the pier that was six feet below the main pier itself. Back in the dark recesses, farthest from the beach, I could hear people laughing and talking. Someone was playing guitar.

Marley led us back there. Giant lights hanging off the pier created weird patterns of light and shadow on the faces of six kids, watching us approach.

"Hey, dudes, this is Amanda-Bliss and Sam-Dean," Marley said by way of introduction. He cocked his head toward a teenage girl sitting cross-legged in a swathe of light. "That's Gina."

She had long black hair, a thin face, and sad eyes. In her lap was a beat-up guitar. She nodded at us.

"They need a place to crash tonight," Marley told her. Evidently she was in charge.

She didn't answer right away. I looked around. In addition to Gina and Marley, there were four other guys and a girl. Three of them were in tattered sleeping bags, two others had ratty blankets laid out like a bed. There were fast-food wrappers strewn around and a box of sugary breakfast cereal was tipped over on its side. A row of skateboards was lined up behind them.

Next to Gina was a small fake Christmas tree, not more than two feet high, strung with seashells. There were a few gifts underneath it, wrapped in old newspaper held by rubber bands. A giant water bug crawled over the presents.

"Dudes, you're kinda young," a guy in a sleeping bag remarked. "Bad scene at home?"

"We're too traumatized to talk about it," Sam said.

"Cops looking for you?" another guy asked sharply.

"We didn't do anything," I said quickly.

"Except run away," Marley said. He crouched down next to the Christmas tree. "Cool tree, Gina."

She smiled. "Thanks." She coughed a few times.

"So, can they stay?" Marley asked her.

"One night," she decided. She coughed again, more deeply this time.

"That's all we need," Sam assured her.

"Are you okay?" I asked her. She sounded kind of sick.

"I'm fine," she said when she'd caught her breath. "You're just little kids. You ought to go home."

"So should you, Mom," a boy in a sleeping bag said.

"This is my home now."

There were murmurs of agreement.

"You have blankets in that backpack?" Gina asked us.

I shook my head no.

Gina turned and looked at the group, waiting. One boy and one girl each pulled off one of their blankets, and handed them to us.

They were so cruddy-looking, I didn't want to take them. But I did. "Thanks," I said. I handed one blanket to Sam. A water bug fell off of it.

"Well, we'll just go sleep down there." I pointed toward the other end of the pier.

"Wait, one thing first," Gina said. She started coughing again, then recovered. "Everyone who stays here has to leave something under our Christmas tree."

I opened the backpack. We didn't have much. I knew Sam didn't want to part with his dancing Elvis sunglasses. I pulled out the two unopened boxes of expensive chocolates and handed them to Gina.

"Whoa, chocolates!" a redheaded kid exclaimed, scrambling out of his sleeping bag. The others gathered around the candy as if they'd just discovered lost gold.

"Just eat one box now," Gina told them. "We're saving the other for Christmas."

"Aw, Mom," the other girl protested. "We're hungry!"

"Too bad. One box of chocolates is plenty for now," Gina decreed firmly, just like a real mother. She smiled at me. "Thanks. Merry Christmas."

"Merry Christmas," I replied.

She strummed a plaintive chord on the guitar. I noticed she was shivering. "Tomorrow night is Christmas Eve. You kids should be home."

"We will be," Sam assured her.

As we walked to the far end of the understructure, Gina began coughing again. I pulled our Elvis sweatshirts out of the backpack and handed one to Sam. "She needs a doctor."

"Agreed."

We both sat down. "They call her Mom."

"I suppose she takes care of them," Sam said.

"But she's just a kid!"

He wrapped himself in one of the cruddy blankets. "You ever think about your mom, Deed? Or your dad? How worried they must be?"

"No," I said, lying cautiously. "Why? Do you?"

"Ed and Sarah Weiss wouldn't do frantic-about-runaway-son very well." He hesitated a moment. "That's why I left them a note."

"You *what*?"

"All it said was that you and I had to go somewhere important, and they shouldn't worry because we'd be back in a few days," Sam explained.

"I'm sure by now they've got the police scouring Disney World."

"Why didn't you tell me you left a note?" I yelled.

Sam huddled in his blanket. "Because I thought you'd react unreasonably, which is exactly how you're reacting. I bet they showed the note to your parents, too."

I opened my mouth to protest.

Sam held up his hand. "This is not a bad thing, Deed. Your parents have been through enough, don't you think?"

"My parents don't care if I live or die."

"Not true."

"True. Ever since it happened, my mom doesn't care about anything. And my father hates me."

"Also not true."

"Real true," I insisted. "He hated me even before I —"

I stopped myself. *Even before I killed David,* I had been about to say. It had almost slipped out.

"Before you what?" Sam asked.

"Never mind."

"*What?*"

"Forget it!" I snapped.

Wrapped in the filthy blankets, we lay down. The smell of the ocean reminded me of last June, the camping trip to Destin, when David had promised to teach me how to swim.

But now, because of me, there was no David.

Every time I remembered, it was as if I were hearing it for the first time. A mortal wound. Fresh. That tight, familiar feeling grabbed my throat. All I could do was hold on, and breathe.

Faint sounds of the guitar filled the air. Gina was playing "We Three Kings of Orient Are." She coughed a few times, then she began to sing in a sweet, clear voice.

> We three kings of Orient are
> Bearing gifts, we travel afar.
> Field and fountain, moor and mountain
> Following yonder star. . . .

I turned onto my stomach, and looked out the end of the pier, searching the sky for Orion, for Betelgeuse. But just when I thought I had found it, clouds moved in and it was gone again.

"Everything changes," I whispered.

"True, Deed. 'Cept for me and you, of course."

He was my best friend, my *only* friend, and sometimes I was so mean to him.

"I'm sorry I got mad before. It's okay that you left a note. It doesn't matter. They won't find us."

"The Great Samdini accepts your apology."

> Star of wonder, star of night
> Star of royal beauty bright . . .

"Sam?"

"What?"

"What do you think happens to a person, after they die?"

A beat of silence. "Dunno."

One star peeked out from behind a cloud. "Wouldn't it be something if people turned into stars, Sam? They'd always be shining on us, and we could always see them."

Now, Gina was singing "White Christmas." Other voices joined in softly.

"Sam, I have to tell you something. You know how you told Gina that we'd be home for Christmas?"

"Uh-huh."

"Well, I won't be."

"Sure you will. Tomorrow morning we'll meet Winston, then we'll call our parents, and by the afternoon we —"

"You don't understand. I'm not going back. Ever."

"All righty, then," Sam joked. "We'll live under the pier with the skateboard family. We'll dine *al fresco* on water bugs. I'll do my *bar mitzvah* on a skateboard."

"I'm serious," I insisted. "I can't go home."

"Of course you can —"

"I *can't*. If you knew what I did . . ."

"What? Oh, I know! You didn't do all the chores on your mother's list. A capital offense."

174

I could hardly breathe. "I did something so terrible."

A beat. And then not a question, but a statement, as Sam realized what I meant.

"This is about David. Isn't it," he decided.

The music stopped. Gina coughed. A big wave slammed into the pier. Everything was dangerous. People got sick. Drowned. Died. Lives changed forever.

I couldn't breathe.

"Deed? What happened that night?"

Breathe in, breathe out, in, out. That was how you stayed alive.

"When you went to the park, what happened?" Sam pressed.

A fist tightened around my heart. I saw stars that weren't in the sky. I had to tell him, someone. I couldn't live with it anymore.

"You can tell me, Deed."

I opened my mouth.

"What happened?"

No words came. Sam would hate me forever if he knew. Everyone would hate me as much as *I* hated me.

"I can't talk about it," I said desperately.

"You *can*, Deed. It can't be so horrible that —"

"I *said* I don't want to talk about it." I scrambled to my feet and gathered the filthy blanket around me. "I'll go and sleep on the beach if you don't shut up!"

Sam stood up, too. "So instead of talking to me you're going to run away from home forever?"

"Yes."

"Class, repeat after me: 'Dee Dee Demento has lost her mind'."

"Shut up, Sam."

"You don't have any place to go! What are you going to do, live here with *them*?" Sam flung his hands toward the skaters. "Pretend Gina is your mom? Marry Marley and skateboard off into the sunset?"

"Maybe!"

"It's stupid, Deed! And I'd never see you again."

"So?"

"*So?*" Sam echoed. "That's all you have to say? *So?*"

We stared at each other, both of us breathing hard. He gathered the blanket around his bony shoulders, and turned to look out toward the dark sea.

"When person A loves person B," he began, "person A gets upset at the thought of never seeing person B again."

He meant me.

He meant he loved me.

But now I knew that love was a poisonous thing. It had turned me into a murderer. I would die with my secret before I would tell.

"It's better that way," I lied, "because person B doesn't love person A back."

He blinked. The moon peeked out from behind the clouds. I watched Sam's face and, in that moment, like a stake driven through a vampire's heart, something died.

It was better that way, too. Now when we split up, he wouldn't feel so bad. Neither would I. Feelings were just a burden that weighed you down. Like a heavy backpack, carrying a copy of some dumb book called *The Member of the Wedding*. Like some stupid journal with newspaper articles about a dead person glued in it.

Silently, we lay back down, and after a while, I fell asleep. I didn't dream. I never did, anymore.

Just one more thing that was better that way.

18

The next morning, we woke up with the sun. Neither of us talked about what we'd said the night before, but it was there between us, like the ocean: deep, dark, too big to see beyond.

By the light of day, the kids who lived under the pier looked terrible. They were dirty. One kid had a black eye. Gina's cough was worse, and spots of red stained her otherwise pale cheeks. I knew that meant she had a fever. When she hugged me good-bye, I wondered what had happened that was so horrible it made her leave home forever.

And then, with a start, I remembered what had happened to me. I laughed in a way that wasn't funny.

Sam and I walked in silence along the beach, back toward Winston's house. The sky was clear, the sun already hot on my shoulders.

"I'm surprised you didn't inform Gina you'd be joining her little family on a permanent basis," he finally said, his voice sour.

"I'll tell her later."

"Rad, dude," Sam said, imitating Marley. "Drop me a postcard when you've panhandled enough money for a stamp."

We were barely on speaking terms. We found a McDonald's, cleaned up in the bathrooms, and ate breakfast in silence. Then we went back to our spot across from Winston Pawling's house.

"Now what?" Sam asked, his mouth set in a hard line.

"We wait. Someone will come out eventually."

Sam gave me a disgusted look. He put on his dancing Elvis sunglasses and looked at his watch. "It's nine o'clock. It is now T-minus-60, and counting. If no one comes out of that house by ten, I'm going over there, I'm knocking on that door, and when someone answers, I'm pointing across the street and telling them who you are."

"You wouldn't do that."

He folded his arms, his face stony. "Yuh. I would."

Across the street, the maid came out and picked up the newspaper that lay in front of the double doors.

"I don't believe it! They're so spoiled, the housekeeper comes on Christmas Eve!"

She turned around to talk to someone I couldn't see. The someone stepped in front of her.

My heart stopped.

The someone was a boy about my age, wearing jeans and a Marlins T-shirt, carrying a football.

179

He was black.

"I guess she isn't the housekeeper," Sam said.

I couldn't speak at all.

What flew into my mind was: My father would *die* if he knew.

And: It isn't fair.

Winston's mom hugged him. Then she told him something I couldn't make out. He nodded. She closed the door. Tossing the football in the air, he started down the street.

Like a magnet was drawing us, we followed him.

Winston headed for the beach, right where we had met Marley the night before. When he got there, five other guys his age were waiting for him. Two were black, two were white, one was brown. Winston was by far the smallest. Awkwardly, he threw the football to the taller black kid. Tossing it between them, they all ran out to the sand.

I stood by the benches, transfixed, watching him. He had almond-shaped eyes. His face lit up when he smiled.

And inside of him was not his heart, but my brother's.

Winston was the worst player of the group. He couldn't throw or catch, but he kept trying.

"Winston, man, you stink!" the brown-skinned kid called in a teasing voice, as Winston dropped another pass and went running after it.

"Nah, Tomas. I'm just holding back so you won't feel bad, man." Winston threw the ball back to him.

Tomas laughed. "Yeah, right. You play worse than my *abuela* back in Cuba!"

"Oooo," the other guys mouthed, laughing at the dis. Winston laughed, too.

The next thing I knew, Sam was heading for the sand. What was he going to do? I started to run after him, then I stopped, panicked.

"Hey," Sam said, as he sauntered over to the group with his best "I'm a bad homie" walk. It was very un-Sam-like. It was also excruciating.

"Yo, what's happening?" Sam asked, loosening up his body in his best "cool" pose.

They all just stared at him.

"So, mind if me and my sister play?"

They examined him like a slide under a microscope.

"What's up with those sunglasses, man?" the smaller black kid finally asked, making a face.

"Oh, these." Sam took off the dancing Elvises and stuck them in his back pocket. "A collectors item. So, we in?"

They looked at one another, considering.

"You any good?" the taller white kid finally asked.

Sam shrugged. "She is." He pointed to me.

They all turned to me, sizing me up.

I felt like barfing.

"Yeah, they call her Dee Dee Demento," Sam went on, as they continued to eye me. "I'm talking NFL, early draft choice."

"Get outta here," the smaller white kid scoffed.

Their assessing eyes were cold and doubting. And they were right. No matter how many hours David had spent teaching me to throw and catch a football in the backyard, that was the me I could be when I was alone with him. I figured winning the stuffed bunny at the carnival had just been dumb luck.

Stutter Girl couldn't play football worth spit.

But then, like a video that had only been partially rewound, a scene popped inside my head from last September. David talking to me and Sam, in my bedroom.

"I just stare their linebackers in the eyes and pretend I'm not scared. Not at all. If I pretend hard enough, Darce, I pretend myself right out of the fear. And run right past them."

Tomas threw me the ball.

I blinked. David was gone. In his place were Winston and his friends, staring at me.

I stared back, right into their eyes, pretending I wasn't scared.

"Go deep!" I called to Winston.

He ran. I waited, waited, and then threw him a beauty. The ball spiraled into the sky and floated down sweetly, right to him.

He caught it without breaking stride, hugging it to my brother's heart.

"Yes!" Winston pumped his right fist in the air. "I *did* it!"

We played for a couple of hours, while the sun rose in the sky. Every twenty minutes or so, Winston had to stop and rest, and one of the other guys would rest with him. When he was playing, he dropped more balls than he caught. Sam played okay. As for me, I threw great pass after great pass. I put everything into it, determined to prove something I couldn't name.

We all finally took a break and plopped down in the sand, wiping our sweaty faces with the bottoms of our T-shirts.

"You're decent," Tomas said to me.

"She's better than you, Hernandez," Winston hooted.

Everyone laughed, teasing him, agreeing.

"So, you guys live around here?" the smaller of the two white kids asked. He had a mouth full of braces.

"We're visiting our grandmother," Sam explained, as he put back on the flying Elvises. "Our parents are in the circus."

"No way," Winston scoffed.

"Yuh way," Sam replied. "The Flying Monellas. I'm Sam-Dean Monella. That's my twin sister, Amanda-Bliss."

Tomas looked at me. "Yo, so why do they call you Dee Dee Demento if your name is Amanda whatever?"

I opened my mouth. Nothing came out.

"See, her full name is Amanda-Bliss-*Deirdre* Monella," Sam explained, "after a lot of dead relatives. Dee Dee for short."

Winston squinted into the sun. "You ever get to travel with the circus?"

"Sure," Sam replied. He told them about being the Great Samdini, the greatest magician and escape artist in the world. "We just did a gig up in Tennessee, actually."

"You're full of it, man," Tomas hooted. He leaned back on his elbows in the sand.

In response, Sam took a quarter out of his pocket, showed it all around, then made it disappear.

"Big deal," the taller black kid, Kenny, said. "My grandfather can make a coin disappear and he's half-blind and crazy. That ain't no Houdini trick."

"As it happens, Houdini did sleight of hand just like this," Sam explained coolly, pocketing the coin. "But I can do a lot of his tricks, big *or* small."

"Oh yeah?" Tomas asked. "Couldn't that Houdini guy pick locks? Well, that's my bike over there." He cocked his head toward the benches. A blue bike was locked to one of them. "If you're telling the truth, pick my bike lock. If you can't, then you're a bald-faced liar."

184

"And we don't like liars," the tall white kid added ominously. His voice had already changed. He sounded like he meant it.

Sam smiled smugly. "Not only could I pick your bike lock with my eyes closed, so can Amanda-Bliss."

They all looked at me.

I walked over to the bike. They all followed me. I felt for the bobby pin in my hair. It was gone. Sam handed me one from his stash.

I knelt down and fitted the bobby pin into the lock. Sam put his hands over my eyes. I moved it so slowly, seeing inside of the lock in my mind's eye, waiting for that perfect click.

And there it was.

I opened the lock. Sam took his hands away from my eyes, so I could hand it to Tomas.

"Awesome! Yo, teach me how to do that!"

"It takes a long time to learn," I said. "Besides, it's not for joking around."

Sam nodded his agreement.

"I gotta get home for lunch," Kenny said. "We got all these boring relatives flying in for Christmas." He rolled his eyes to show what he thought of it.

The others said they had to go, too.

"Hey, you want to come over to my house for lunch?" Tomas asked us eagerly. "You gotta show that trick to my dad. He'll freak."

"Nah," I said. "Thanks, though."

Kenny threw the football to Winston, who said good-bye to everyone, including us, and started to walk away. His friends went off in different directions.

I wanted to stop Winston. I opened my mouth. No sound came out. What could I say?

"Hey, wait up!" Sam called, running to catch him. I trotted after him.

"Listen," Sam said, walking along with Winston, "I was wondering. We have these special medical problems in the circus. I was thinking possibly we could ask your parents for some advice."

"What, like now?" Winston asked.

Sam nodded.

"How'd you know my parents are doctors?" Winston asked.

"Our grandmother sees your mom," Sam said, before I could stop him.

Winston laughed. "You got the wrong doctor. My mom's a pediatrician — you know, a kid doctor. My dad runs a public health clinic, but it's on the other side of Miami."

"Did I say our grandmother saw your mother?" Sam asked. "I meant the *grandchildren* of our grandmother. Our cousins. The Monella kids, Barbarella and Mandella Monella. Right, Amanda-Bliss-Deirdre?"

I nodded.

Winston laughed. "You sure got some weird names in your family." He scratched his chin, considering. "My parents are kind of busy right now. Getting ready for Christmas and like that."

"We won't stay long," Sam promised.

Winston thought for a minute. "If you were to come over, you wouldn't need to say anything about how I was actually playing football just now."

"We wouldn't," Sam agreed.

Winston shrugged. "Yeah, then. Okay."

Okay. Just like that.

Winston Pawling was taking us home.

19

The three of us walked along together.

"So, you a big football fan?" Sam asked, shaking his hair off his face.

"Yeah," Winston said. "Me and my dad used to go to all the 'Canes home games."

Sam looked at him blankly.

"University of Miami? Hurricanes? I thought your grandma lives here."

"She does," Sam said. "But, see, she just moved here. From . . . Disney World!

"What, you mean Orlando?" Winston asked.

"Yuh, that's it. Sis and I are just getting to know the lay of the land. Right, Amanda-Bliss-Deirdre?"

"Call me Dee Dee," I said through clenched teeth.

Winston looked at me and shook his head. "That's a whole lot of names you've got."

"It's a . . . family thing," I managed.

"Yeah, mine, too." He threw the football into the

air and caught it. "Winston was my grandfather's name. Kids are always asking was I named after a pack of cigarettes. I'm like, 'Both my parents are doctors. What do *you* think?'"

"Do you want to be a doctor, too?" Sam asked.

"Not me, man. I spent enough time in hospitals to last me a lifetime."

"Yeah? How come?" Sam asked innocently.

"Oh, I was born with my heart kinda messed up. So I had to have this surgery."

We had just about reached his house. Now, now it would happen. He would tell us about his heart transplant, about a hero named David Deeton, only eighteen years old, who had given him his heart. About how that heart was beating inside of him right that minute, keeping him alive, giving him life. About how he owed his life to David Deeton.

We walked up the front walkway.

"So, what happened?" Sam finally asked, as we got to the front door.

"So . . . I'm fine now," Winston said. "Come on."

I was too stunned to move. He wasn't grateful at all! He had never given my brother one moment's thought.

He probably didn't even know David' name.

Fury bubbled up inside of me. I went inside. Sam was already waiting in the huge front hall. The high ceiling was sloped like the cathedral ceiling at church.

"Where's *Winston*?" I said his name with a nasty edge.

"He went to tell his parents he brought home company."

I looked around. To the left, down a few steps, was a sunken living room. The expensive furniture was perfect-looking, like no one actually used it. There was a grand piano with a vase of fresh flowers on it, and family photos. In a corner, on a pedestal, was a black marble sculpture of a woman cradling her baby. The polished wooden floor gleamed around the edges of a tapestry rug, which lay in front of a two-story-high slate-gray fireplace.

In front of the picture window was the huge Christmas tree I had seen from across the street. It was strung with the most beautiful ornaments, no two alike. Underneath the tree were colorfully wrapped presents of every size and shape.

My family didn't have a Christmas tree. *My* family didn't have presents.

Winston came down the hall with his parents. Up close, I could see that his mother was beautiful, with high cheekbones, and Winston's almond-shaped eyes. His father was tall and broad-shouldered. Both of them wore jeans and the kind of expensive sweaters my parents couldn't afford.

"Hello," his mom said cordially. "I'm Linda

Pawling, Winston's mother. This is Winston's dad, John Paul Pawling."

Winston's father nodded at us. "I understand you two are here in Miami visiting your grandmother."

Sam nodded. "I'm Sam-Dean Monella. This is my sister, Amanda-Bliss-Deirdre."

Winston laughed and nudged his father. "I told you it was worse than Winston." His dad gave him a playful wink.

His mother tapped her finger on her chin. "Wait. Haven't I seen you two before?"

And then it hit me. The candy scam! How could Sam and I have both forgotten?

"Yesterday. We were selling candy for school," I reminded her, since I knew she'd figure it out anyway.

She snapped her fingers. "That's right! But I thought you said you were selling candy for school. So if you're visiting your grandmother —"

"Oh, well, when you're show-biz kids like we are, it gets complicated," Sam interrupted. "See, sometimes we're with the circus. But other times, we're with Granny."

Winston's parents both looked skeptical, but they were too polite to say anything.

"Well, we were just about to have a light lunch, if you kids would like to join us?" his mom asked.

"How delightful," Sam replied.

We went through the sunken living room to an attached dining room, where sliding glass doors led out to the backyard patio. Beyond the patio was a gleaming, kidney-shaped, built-in swimming pool, and beyond that was one of the oddest things I had ever seen in my life.

Circling the middle of a palm tree, like a huge wooden doughnut, was a tree house. The roof was thatched, the floor made of plywood. Green-and-white-striped awnings hung down as walls. There was a ladder up one side, on the other side was a wooden platform attached by thick ropes that ran all the way up to the tree house. There were pulleys at the bottom and top of the ropes.

"Intense," Sam said.

"Cool, huh? My dad built it," Winston said proudly.

"Winston helped," his father said, putting his arm around his son's shoulders. "It was quite a project."

Sam was dazzled in a very un-Sam-like way. Something about that made my hands clench into fists.

"I'll just get a couple more table settings," Mrs. Pawling said. "You kids can sit down."

We sat around a large redwood picnic table. There were big bowls of tuna salad, fresh fruit salad, and sliced avocados and tomatoes. David had loved avocados.

We hardly ever had them. *We* couldn't afford them.

"So," Winston's dad said, "you all met at the beach this morning?"

"Yes, sir," Sam said, "playing touch football. Winston is a really good player."

Winston shot Sam a fierce look.

"Son?" his father asked, raising his eyebrows. "Didn't you promise your mother?"

"He didn't actually play," Sam added quickly, realizing his error. "Did I make it sound like he played? He threw the ball maybe once. Twice at the most."

"At the very most," Winston agreed, nodding.

His dad made a fist and playfully hit Winston in his bicep. "Hang in there, son. In another two or three months, you'll be out there struttin' your stuff, back at school, the whole deal."

"Don't tell Mom I played, okay?" Winston asked, his voice low.

His father nodded.

Winston's mom came back with two more table settings, and a whole bunch of pills on a tray. She handed the pills to Winston, who turned his back to us and swallowed them quickly with a glass of water, as if he was embarrassed we were watching.

"So, tell us about the circus," his mom said, passing bowls of food around the table.

Sam took huge helpings of everything and eagerly went into his Flying Monellas story. It got more and more elaborate every time he told it. I just sat there silently. All I took was the tiniest bit of tuna salad, which I pushed around on my plate.

So what if Winston took a lot of pills and wasn't supposed to do sports yet? In a couple of months he'd be fine, and his parents would be so happy. But my parents would never be fine or happy again *ever*.

My stomach grumbled hungrily, and I looked down at the tuna salad on my plate.

No way was I eating their food.

"We're thinking of staying with the circus on a full-time basis next year," Sam was saying. He took a sip of his fresh-squeezed orange juice. "We'd leave Marlins Middle School and just have tutors. My idea of perfection is to never have to go to school again."

"You wouldn't feel like that if you couldn't go," Winston said, shrugging.

"Why can't you go to school?" I blurted out, my voice too loud.

Say it, I willed Winston, staring at him hard. *Say it.* No one answered me.

"Winston went to Holy Trinity when he was younger," his dad finally said. "He'll be back there in the spring. All his friends go there, too. I guess you met some of them at the beach this morning. Those kids have been tight since they were in preschool together."

Winston's mom smiled at him. "You have such great friends. They've really stood by you."

Winston got up abruptly, like he was embarrassed. "Hey, want to see my room?"

"Maybe your guests aren't done eating," his mom said. She looked at my plate, then at me, a question in her eyes.

"Thank you, I'm not very hungry," I said stiffly.

"Come on," Winston said.

We followed him down a hallway to his room. It was at least three times as big as my room, with wall-to-wall carpeting, bunk beds, a CD-player, and a big-screen TV. One wall was lined with books, and there were boxes of games on the bottom of some shelves. In the corner on a desk was a *kinara*, which holds the candles that get lit, one for each night of Kwanzaa. I knew about Kwanzaa because of book #16 on Meemaw's list: *A Very Special Kwanzaa*. Next to that was an incredible Compaq computer with a color printer next to it; both of them major upgrades from Sam's.

The computer was the exact model I wanted and would never, ever have.

Sam looked around, stunned. "Your parents really should consider adopting me."

Winston turned on his computer. Soon he had it booted up to a CD-ROM game. An intergalactic warrior had to fight his way through an increasingly difficult maze of evil extraterrestrials. I said I didn't want to play. Sam, who is great at computer games, couldn't get past level three. Winston got to level six.

"Excellent," Sam told him, clearly impressed. "How'd you get so good?"

"I had a lot of time to practice," Winston said.

Next they turned on the big-screen TV. Some football game was on. Winston and Sam plopped down on the carpet.

"Cop a squat, Amanda-Bliss-Deirdre," Sam said. "What a great chance this would be to *talk*." He gave me a significant look and cocked his head at Winston.

I sat. "I don't have anything to *say*."

For a while Sam kept looking over at me, like why didn't I say something, but finally he gave up. Winston pulled out a Gameboy — another thing I wanted badly and didn't have — and the two of them alternated playing Tetris while they watched football.

I just sat there, getting madder and madder. Winston had everything: two great parents who loved him, money, friends, even Sam, it felt like.

And he had David, too.

It wasn't fair. He didn't even appreciate any of it.

His dad knocked on the open bedroom door. "Winston, you need to start getting ready, son. It's nearly three and we're leaving for mass at four o'clock sharp."

Mrs. Pawling came up next to her husband. "I'm

sure your friends need to get back to their grand-mother's, since it's Christmas Eve."

"Oh, no," Sam said breezily, "we're Jewish." He thought a minute. "Monella is an Italian name, of course. Because we're . . . Italian Jews. There are some, you know."

Linda Pawling looked amused. "Yes, I had heard that. I hope you'll excuse Winston, because he needs to get changed for —"

"Church." My voice was tight and low. "So you can pray, and give thanks for your blessings. But you never really think about who suffered for your blessings, do you."

A warm smile came to Linda's lips. "Oh, but I do. I thank Jesus every time I look at my son's face."

Winston looked embarrassed. "Hey!" he said suddenly. "Didn't you have some kind of medical question you wanted to ask my parents?"

"*She* does," Sam said. He looked pointedly at me.

Now, his eyes said. *Tell them now.*

Winston was standing with his parents. His dad put his arm around Winston's shoulders, his mom smiled warmly. There they were, the three of them, this perfect, little family unit on Christmas Eve, on their way to church, where they would thank God and Jesus, but they never gave one tiny little thought to my brother. There would be no prayers for David, or for the Deeton family.

I could feel my hate for them growing, bubbling up inside of me like molten lava, clouding my vision, my mind. Now it seemed to me that the Pawlings had *stolen* their happiness from my family. After all, who were the Deetons, anyway? Just some white family in some small town in Wisconsin, who didn't have enough money, whose dad had lost out on his promotion to a black man. They probably hated white people as much as my dad now seemed to hate black people.

The Pawlings stood there, waiting for me to speak.

"Sis?" Sam prompted me.

I looked away. "Never mind. It wasn't important."

"Do you kids need a ride to your grandmother's?" Mrs. Pawling asked. "What street does she live on?"

Sam's eyes locked on me. "I really think that Amanda-Bliss-Deirdre has something to tell you."

"No," I said.

"Yes." Sam walked over to me.

"It doesn't matter."

"It *does* matter. Tell them."

Sam waited for me to speak. I cut my eyes at him.

Quit pushing me, I thought. *I hate you, too. I hate everybody.*

"Here's how you start," Sam said slowly, ignoring my cold, angry eyes. "My name isn't really Amanda-Bliss-Deirdre."

He reached for my hand. I pulled it away.

"She's not really my sister, either," he said, his eyes still locked on mine.

"I don't understand," Mrs. Pawling said.

"Winston, do you know what's going on here?" his father asked sharply.

"Nah." He shrugged, bewildered.

"Tell them, Deed," Sam said.

"No."

"You have to."

"No!" was torn from some place so deep inside of me, I didn't even know it existed.

"*Tell* them," Sam insisted. "You can do it. My name is . . ."

I turned my back on him.

"My name is . . ." Sam said. "My name is . . ."

I put my hands over my ears. "Shut up!"

"My name is . . ."

"Shut up, Sam! Shut up!"

But he wouldn't. "My name is . . . my name is . . . my name is . . ."

Something inside me snapped, gave way. I swung around, wild-eyed, out of control.

"My name is Darcy Deeton!" I screamed at the Pawlings. "My brother was David Deeton. But you don't even know who that is, do you?"

Winston's mother gasped, and clapped her hand

to her mouth. Her husband put his arm around her.

My whole body was shaking. "You all live here in your perfect house with your perfect pool and your perfect computer and your perfect Christmas and your perfect lives. And you don't even know! You don't even know!"

Viciously, I swiped my arm across Winston's desk, knocking things to the floor.

I swung around, and pointed at Winston. "You! You took everything from my family. Do you know what they have? Nothing! *Nothing!* And you have everything! You're only alive because of my brother. You have his heart. *And you don't even know his name.*"

Winston's jaw hung open. His mother took a step toward me. She held out her arms.

"No!" I screamed savagely. "Stay away from me!"

"But I know how much you're hurting," she said, tears in her eyes. She moved toward me again.

"You don't know *anything!*" I screamed. "I *deserve* to hurt! I deserve to *die!*"

"Deed —" Sam began.

"I do. Because I killed him."

The room was hushed. I backed into a corner, my fingers splayed against the wall. There was no place left to go, no place to hide.

And the voice in my head, the one I had come to hate, whispered: *It isn't the Pawlings who robbed your family of happiness.*

It was you.

Suddenly, I wasn't in Winston's room anymore. I was back in Houdini Park. It was that night, all over again.

"Today's my birthday," I whispered. "David went to the park with the J-Word. I hate her but David loves her. I was so mean to her. I want to apologize. So I sneak out of the house and go to the park. There they are, sitting on a bench, kissing. They don't see me.

"Jayne is saying something. About the necklace David gave me for my birthday — that it was her idea, not his. I'm so mad. I tear my necklace off and throw it at him. *'I hate you! I wish you were dead!'* I'm running, running, running away, David is running after me. I hear him call to me, but I won't stop. I want him to hurt! Like he hurt me. I want to make him sorry."

Tears streamed down my face. I slid down the wall.

"I'm running faster, out of the park, across the street. Now David runs across the street because I did, between the parked cars, after me, and there's a terrible sound, a terrible sound. A car, a thud, a crash. I can't turn around. *Oh, God, I can't turn around*!"

Mrs. Pawling had her arms around me.

"I killed him," I sobbed. "Don't be nice to me. Please. I want to die. I deserve to die."

I never heard anyone leave, but she must have told them to, because suddenly we were alone.

"Shhhh," she crooned, rocking me in her arms. I felt her tears on my cheek, mingling with mine. "Poor baby. It's okay, baby. It's okay now."

"I didn't mean to," I sobbed. "Please, God, I didn't mean to."

"I know," she crooned, holding me tight. "And God knows, too, baby. I believe that with all my heart. You can lay your burden down now. God knows. And He forgives."

"You don't understand," I whispered. "It's not God I need to forgive me. It's David."

20

There was just something about Linda Pawling that made me feel as if I could tell her anything, everything, and she wouldn't hate me. So I did.

About my dad and how he lost out on his promotion to Charles Jordan.

About how my father had changed, and how he said these ugly things about black people even though he hadn't raised us up to be like that at all.

About Dad's back.

About Meemaw.

About our search for David's heart.

I told it all.

Mrs. Pawling just listened, sometimes stroking my hair, sometimes just nodding. When I was through, she got me a clean T-shirt, helped me to undress, and put me to bed in the bottom bunk. Then she kissed my forehead, and turned out the light.

I never thought I would sleep, but I did.

When I woke up, groggy and confused, it was nighttime. My clothes had been freshly washed, they were laying on the chair. I put them on and sat on the bed, thinking. Now that the Pawlings and Sam knew what I had done, it was only a matter of time before my parents found out. How could I ever face them?

I thought about Gina, sick and shivering under the pier. Could I really be like her and run away forever? Could I live with the skaters under the pier, pretend they were my family, pretend Gina was my mom?

It gave me a horrible, lonely feeling in the pit of my stomach. I had a real mom, and I loved her.

I just wasn't sure she would still love me back.

I followed the sounds of recorded Christmas carols to the spacious family room. Winston and Sam were sitting on the carpet at the marble coffee table, playing chess. I noticed Sam's clothes were clean, too, and so was Sam. His hair was still wet, combed off his face in a very un-Sam-like fashion.

"Hi." I stared at the rug.

They both said hi back.

I couldn't look at them. "I fell asleep, I guess. So, where are your parents?"

"Dad's in the bedroom," Winston said. "Mom's at church."

I scratched my arm. "I ruined your Christmas Eve."

"Nah," Winston said. "You hungry or anything? Mom said to ask."

I shook my head yes, and dug my sneaker into the thick carpeting. I didn't know what to do with myself.

"Be right back." Winston disappeared in the direction of the kitchen.

Sam came over to me. "I called home, Deed. My dad hyperventilated. Bette had to get him to breathe into a paper bag."

He waited for me to smile.

I didn't.

He hesitated. "You're about to get extremely angry. I . . . called your house, too. I talked to your dad."

I shrugged. "Your parents would have called them, anyway."

"That wasn't the 'extremely angry' part. I told your dad the truth about what happened."

Oh, God. Oh, no. They would hate me.

"You can say I didn't have any right to tell," Sam rushed on, "and I didn't. But I knew you'd run away forever before you'd tell. I couldn't let you do it even if it means you hate me."

"What did my father say?"

"Not much," Sam admitted.

Winston came back with an open bag of chips and some granola bars stuck in the pocket of his T-shirt. "My parents got you guys a flight home tomorrow."

Winston held out the chips to me, but I had lost my appetite. My father knew the truth now. And my mom. And Andy. How could I go back home and face them all?

How?

"We can't afford a plane," I told Winston.

"My parents said it was a gift." He put the chips down, and buried his hands deep in the pockets of his jeans. "Um . . . there's something I kind of wanted to show you."

He took us outside to the backyard, which was now illuminated by floodlights. We stood under the tree house, looking up.

"My dad built it when I was nine," Winston said, "right after I had my first surgery to try and fix my heart. I was so sick. I couldn't do anything — run around, play sports, finally I couldn't even go to school. So I just laid out here, too tired to move, watching my dad build this. Every day, he'd say to me: 'Lookin' good today, son. You're gettin' stronger. By the time I'm done building this, you'll be strong enough to climb up the ladder to your own tree house.'"

Winston shook his head. "He was wrong. I wasn't strong enough. I thought it was my fault. And I felt so bad, that I'd let him down."

He pointed to the wooden platform attached to two heavy ropes. "Sit there," he told Sam.

Sam sat.

Winston cocked his head for me to follow him. We went to the other side of the tree and the two of us pulled on two other ropes. Slowly, the platform lifted, until Sam was level to the tree house.

"When I was sick that's how I used to get up there," Winston explained.

"Excellent," Sam called down.

"Except I had to blow a whistle to get someone to come use the pulley to get me down again," Winston told Sam. "Go on in."

Sam crawled into the tree house.

Winston scrambled up the ladder ahead of me. He didn't have any trouble at all. He turned on a giant flashlight. Now I could see that the palm tree in the center of the tree house was covered with a bunch of framed photos.

"These are my all-time heroes," Winston explained. "That's Jackie Robinson. That's Guy Bluford, Jr. — he was the first black astronaut in space. That's Michael Jordan — well, I guess you know who he is. And that's David Deeton."

There was a framed photo of my brother, in his football uniform, his helmet under his arm, grinning into the camera. With one finger, I touched the glass over my brother's smile.

David.

"When I got my transplant, my parents found out whose heart I had," Winston went on. "Then they tracked down a newspaper article about your brother, with this photo. Mom framed it and put it next to my hospital bed. When I came home, it came home, too."

"You could have written to us," I said. "You could have thanked my parents. Something."

"Yeah." Winston looked down at his hands. "You know my friends — you met them. They're great. But when I was sick, they treated me different. You know, like I was the weird sick kid. It was like ... like they were still my friends, but we lived on different planets or something. Man, I hated that so much.

"I used to lie up here and make deals with God. Like, if God would give me one year to be normal, like my friends, just *one*, I'd give Him anything He wanted."

"Petitioning with prayer," Sam said, nodding.

"It didn't work," Winston said "I just got sicker. I was Status One for a heart transplant. That means you're so sick you have to live at the hospital, and you go to the top of the list. But you have to be a tissue match with the donor. Ten people die every day, waiting for an organ that never comes."

He turned off the flashlight. Moonlight streamed in through the thatching of the roof.

"I knew I was dying," Winston went on. "My parents told me to pray. But what was the point? I had already offered God a sweet deal, and He turned me down."

"And then you got David's heart," I said softly.

Winston nodded. "They didn't tell me whose it was until later. But when I woke up after the surgery, and I felt his heart beating inside of me, I knew. He was young. And strong. I never felt that way before. Never."

I drew my knees up to my chest. "You could write to my parents now. It's not too late."

"It's hard for me to . . ." Winston began. Then he stopped, and began again. "On New Year's Day, the last night of Kwanzaa, I'm giving a speech in church about David, and *Imani*."

"Definition, please," Sam asked.

"*Imani* is the seventh principle of Kwanzaa," Winston explained. "Faith." He glanced at me quickly. "My parents asked me, did I want to write to your parents? But I said no. It didn't seem right. I was so happy to be alive. And their son was dead. I thought that they would hate me."

The air was still and silent. What if he was right?

Then, Winston spoke again. "I just want you to know," he went on, "that I think about David all the time. *All* the time."

In the moonlight I saw Winston quickly brush the tears from his cheek. I pretended not to see, and lay on my back, gazing out through an opening in the tree house walls, up at the night sky. Sam and Winston lay down, too.

My eyes searched, following the starry landmarks Meemaw had taught me.

And there it was.

"See that red star?" I pointed to the sky. "That's Betelgeuse. It's 527 light-years from Earth. Even if it died tonight, its light would keep on shining for the next 527 years."

I looked over at Winston's tear-streaked face, as he squinted and tried to find Betelgeuse.

"Winston? Could I listen to my brother's heart?"

The question hung in the air, suspended.

Slowly, Winston nodded.

Ever so gently, I put my head down on his chest. And then, under my right ear, I heard the beating of my brother's heart.

Bu-bum. Bu-bum. Bu-bum.

Strong and steady and sure, it beat, just like David.

"Can you hear it, Deed?" Sam asked, his voice hushed.

Tears streamed down my face, but there was a smile of wonder on my lips.

"It's so wonderful, Sam. It's wonderful!"

Bu-bum. Bu-bum. Bu-bum.

"I love you, David," I whispered. "And I miss you. So much. I'll remember everything you taught me for the next 527 years. Someday I'll teach it to my children, and they'll teach it to their children, so your light will never go out. Thank you for being the greatest brother in the world.

And most of all, thank you for saving Winston's life."

Bu-bum. Bu-bum. Bu-bum.

I lay there with my head on Winston's chest, absolutely still, my mind cleared of everything, just like Sam when he sat under the Metamorphosis statue and communed with the spirit of Houdini. Call me crazy, but as I listened to the beating of David's heart, I felt his spirit surround me with love, and I heard his gentle voice, not with my ears and not with my mind, but with my heart:

"Darce," he said, "I forgive you."

21

I stared out the window of the plane. Already Miami seemed far away. Just two nights ago we had slept under a pier with a bunch of runaways.

"I'm glad Winston's parents called Dr. Levy to check on that girl Gina," I told Sam. "It's not like we knew she had pneumonia."

"Agreed."

"Ladies and gentlemen, we are making our final approach to Green Bay. Please make sure your safety belts are securely fastened, and all seats are in the upright position. We'll be on the ground shortly. Thank you."

My stomach did a flip-flop.

"Nervous?" Sam asked me.

"Beyond."

"You need a talisman," Sam said.

"In English that would be . . . ?"

"'Noun. An object that is supposed to bring good luck.'" He reached into his pocket and offered me the dancing Elvis sunglasses.

I was touched. "They're your favorite thing in the world."

"Correct," Sam said, still holding them out to me.

"Thanks, anyway." I stared out the window again. "You know that necklace David gave me? The one Jayne picked out?"

"The heart?"

I nodded. "I really, really wish I still had that." I thought a minute. "Jayne wasn't so terrible, Sam. She was nice."

"Here's a concept: tell her," Sam suggested.

I stared out the window some more. Sam took out a red pen and doodled something or other, but I didn't pay any attention. I was so scared. As the plane descended, so did my courage.

We were on the ground.

"Welcome to Green Bay," the flight attendant said over the intercom. "As you can see, we've got a white Christmas here in Wisconsin. Dress warm, and happy holidays, folks."

As the plane taxied to the gate, through the window I saw fat snowflakes dance toward the ground. Spirits in the plane were high. Several rows behind us, two little kids sang "Jingle Bells."

I can do this, I can do this, I can do this, I chanted to myself, as Sam and I walked off the plane.

The first people I saw were Sam's parents and Bette. They ran to him and he disappeared in their welcoming arms.

213

"You are grounded until your wedding day," his father said, as he hugged Sam fiercely, tears in his eyes.

I looked around. There were no welcoming arms for me. It was stupid for me to hope that they'd come to the —

And then, there he was.

My father. Standing near the wall.

And Mom. And Andy. Staring at me, like they were on the other side of an ocean no one knew how to cross.

I just stood there, so scared, so lonely.

"Hey, Demento!"

I looked up. Sam had pushed out of his family's embrace. He held up one palm. And on it, he had doodled a huge, red heart, just like the heart David had given me.

I had to smile. Sam is such a moron.

I closed my eyes. Even though there was noise all around me, Christmas carols, excited voices, I was perfectly still. And in the stillness, I heard David's voice again.

I have faith in you, Darce. Go to them. They are the we of you.

I opened my eyes, and turned toward my family.

Metamorphosis. Noun. A change of form or character, I thought. *If you believe in yourself, and just put one foot in front of the other, and you keep doing it, you can learn to walk, run a marathon, even spread your wings and, for the very first time, you can fly.*

I stood in front of my family. "I'm sorry I worried you. I love you, Mom." I looked at Andy. "I even love you."

Mom's arms opened. Wordlessly, she held me close. Andy even gave me a quick hug.

Then I turned to my father and looked into his eyes. And the strangest thing happened — for the first time, I saw him the way David saw him. Instead of thinking about all the things he *didn't* give me, I thought about all the things he *did*.

Like the year he carved me a wooden doll house for my birthday.

Like the time I saw a scary movie and he checked for monsters under my bed every single night for a month.

Like the day he came to school with me in uniform, and he told my class that being a police officer meant you would risk your own life to protect others. And he meant it.

Like a hero.

I reached for my father's hand.

"I have something for you, Daddy. I brought you your Christmas present."

I turned around. There were the Pawlings, and Winston, waiting behind me. They had changed all of their plans for Christmas and flown to Wisconsin with us, even knowing the horrible things my father had said about black people. Not knowing if my parents would hate Winston for being alive when David was not.

I had asked them to do it. I don't know how I had gotten up the nerve, but I had.

And they had said yes.

I went to Winston, and took his arm. He gave a quick look to his parents, and they nodded at him. Then, hand-in-hand, Winston and I walked over to my father.

"Daddy, this is my friend, Winston. He has David's heart."

My father began to tremble. One large, rough hand reached out to cup Winston's cheek. Then the tall white man with the bad back who had blamed all of his bad luck on a black man, knelt down and tenderly held the short black kid who had his son's heart.

Winston hesitated a moment. Then he lifted his arms, and gently wrapped them around my father. And he put his head on my father's shoulder.

"Thank you," my father said. "Dear God, thank you."

If anyone had stopped to watch us, they might have found it funny to see what happened next: a white Lutheran family and a white Jewish family and a black Catholic family all hugging one another in the Green Bay airport, crying together. All around us people were hurrying to their own families, to the places they belonged. It was just like what Frankie had called it in *The Member of the Wedding*.

The we of me.

Everyone needs a we of me. Everyone.

Winston was on one side of me, Sam on the other. Sam gave me a very Sam-like grin, and put his hand with the big, red heart on it in mine.

Then my father reached out, and put his arms around all three of us, Winston, me, Sam. I felt his tears on my cheek. "I love you, Dee Dee," he said. "With all my heart."

"I know."

And deep in my heart, I finally did.

"Merry Christmas, Daddy."

He smiled through his tears. "Merry Christmas, Dee Dee. Merry Christmas."

Epilogue

It was many hours later. Sam, Winston, and I walked silently down the halls of Appleton Acres. It was as quiet as a tomb. Under a "Merry Christmas" banner, a huge cutout of Santa riding his sleigh had come partly unglued from the wall. At the nurses' desk, an electric Hanukkah menorah glowed for the sixth night of Hanukkah.

I pushed the door open to Meemaw's room. She lay on her back, sightless, the same as always. The fresh Christmas flowers my parents had brought over that morning were on her nightstand.

I asked the night nurse to leave us alone for a while, and I pulled a chair up to the bed. "It's almost midnight, Meemaw," I said. "I brought some friends to see you. You know Sam. And this is my new friend, Winston."

I took Meemaw's hand. "Betelgeuse is out tonight. I wish you could see it. I just showed Dad. He's waiting out in the car. I asked him to bring me over. I wanted to see you while it's still Christmas.

"I know you must be wondering why David stopped coming to see you. I'm sorry to have to tell you this, Meemaw, but David is dead. He was in an accident. I miss him so much. I know you do, too."

I choked a little and felt myself start to cry, and looked over at Winston and Sam. They pulled two chairs up next to me.

"You okay?" Winston asked softly.

I took a deep breath. "K-O," I replied. I turned back to my grandmother. "In one way, Meemaw, David will never die. Because his heart is still beating, right this minute, inside Winston. David saved Winston's life. Isn't that a miracle? Blink once if you can hear me, Meemaw."

We waited.

She didn't blink.

My eyes went to the photo of her above her bed, from when she was young. The one that looked like me. It didn't scare me anymore.

"Just one more thing, Meemaw. I started book number twenty-eight, *The Member of the Wedding*. I lost my copy before I could finish it — it's a long story — but Winston's mom — she's a doctor, her name is Linda Pawling — gave me hers."

I pulled the worn paperback out of my back pocket. "My friends and I thought we'd kind of catch you up on the first part tonight, and then when I come back to see you, I can read a little more each time, and then you and I can read the end together. Okay?"

We waited again. There was no reaction at all.

But that was okay. Faith is when your heart tells you something is true even if you can't prove it. That's what David believed.

As for me, I was pretty much convinced that Meemaw wasn't there. The truth was, I didn't have David's faith.

But I did have the greatest gift of all: his heart.

And so with Sam on one side of me, and Winston on the other, I slowly opened *The Member of the Wedding*. And just before the clock struck midnight, while it was still the time of miracles, I began to read.